# THE WORLD OF JONNY BRIGGS

'Surely I didn't hear the word RABBIT HUTCH?' Jonny Briggs's mother said accusingly. 'Surely no one is hinting at the presence of a RABBIT around this place?'

But this is *exactly* what Jonny Briggs is hinting at, though he hadn't meant his mam to overhear! And that's not the only thing he's keen to complicate life with; his sudden interest in making gingerbread men and kites is bound to bring chaos – and fun – to the lives of those around him . . .

*The following titles by Joan Eadington are also available from BBC/Knight*

Jonny Briggs
Jonny Briggs and the Ghost
Jonny Briggs and the Whitby Weekend
Jonny Briggs and the Great Razzle Dazzle
Jonny Briggs and the Giant Cave
Jonny Briggs and the Galloping Wedding
Jonny Briggs and the Jubilee Concert

# THE WORLD OF JONNY BRIGGS

## Joan Eadington

*Illustrated by William Marshall*

BBC/KNIGHT

Copyright © Joan Eadington 1985
Illustrations © British Broadcasting Corporation 1985
*First published 1985 by British Broadcasting Corporation/Knight Books*

**British Library C.I.P.**

Eadington, Joan
    The world of Jonny Briggs.
    I. Title    II. Marshall, William
    823'.914[J]    PZ7

    ISBN 0–340–38718–1
        (0 563 20423 0) BBC

The front cover shows Richard Holian as Jonny Briggs in the BBC television series, which was dramatised by Valerie Georgeson and Joan Eadington, produced by Angela Beeching and directed by Christine Secombe.

*The characters and situations in this book are entirely imaginary and bear no relation to any real person or actual happening*

Printed and bound in Great Britain for The British Broadcasting Corporation, 35 Marylebone High Street, London W1M 4AA and Hodder and Stoughton Paperbacks, a division of Hodder and Stoughton Ltd., Mill Road, Dunton Green, Sevenoaks, Kent (Editorial Office: 47 Bedford Square, London WC1B 3DP) by Richard Clay (The Chaucer Press) Ltd, Bungay, Suffolk

# Contents

# 1
# The Book Battle

Jonny Briggs was being invisible. He was standing like a foggy statue in front of the classroom bookshelf. He'd put on his most faded trousers that morning and his least white T-shirt, so as to keep unseen.

He hardly dared to breathe as he stared at the books: yes – it was still there! Sometimes it vanished for ages.

And now, he wanted it to vanish again ... But this time to his own bedroom at home. It was to be a special secret between him and Pam Dean that the twins wouldn't know about ...

He moved his fingers gently towards the title on its bright, white spine without even moving his elbows. Nobody else in the class seemed the least bit bothered. They were all yackety-yacketing about making ginger biscuits and being cooks.

The book was huge. All the others looked really titchy beside it. The picture on the front was beautiful – a very big orange carrot and a fat white rabbit munching it. The title, in red, was *Rabbit Care*.

"Just like the *school* rabbit," breathed Jonny, "pink eyes an' all." He took one swift, sweeping, sidelong glance then, with a mighty grab, tugged the book from its cramped resting place, pushed it up his T-shirt and folded his arms over the top – just in time to hear all the rest of the books thundering to the floor like a collapsing castle! The attention of the whole class was upon him ...

"What on earth is going on?" cried Miss Broom, who was busy helping the Brown brothers to unwedge a paint brush from the hinge of a mouse trap which they'd found at home.

"*He's* going on! That's what it is, miss," said Josie, one of the twins, in triumph. "He's not copied down a single ginger-nut recipe. He's just plain lazy. He's a disgrace to our class."

"Please, Miss Broom – he's got something stuffed up his T-shirt. He's never as big as that at the top ..." squeaked Jinny, the other twin.

Chants of *Incredible Bulk*, and *Oompah, oompah – stick it oop ya joompah* filled the air as Jonny dodged back to his desk.

"Come back here IMMEDIATELY," ordered Miss Broom. "Pick up all those books this instant and put them back in their proper order, *including* the one hidden under your T-shirt ..."

Thirty pairs of sharp, probing eyes watched in hushed silence. It was one of those days when hardly anyone was absent.

Slowly, Jonny returned to the bookshelf and clumsily tried to slip the rabbit book back to the shelf unseen whilst picking up the rest.

"It was THE RABBIT BOOK, Miss Broom," yelled Josie, pink with glee. "He was pinching it!"

Miss Broom sighed quietly: "There's no such thing as pinching books from that shelf, Josie. All of you can borrow them as long as you give your names to the class librarian." Miss Broom looked round enquiringly: "Who is the class librarian for this week?"

Slowly, Pam put her hand up: "I am, Miss Broom. And he's not pinched it. I've written it down. He told me he was getting it."

Miss Broom nodded briskly. "Right – take the book back to your desk, Jonny. And look after it properly. Remember – all of you – that most of these extra special books are on loan from the town library." Then she said: "And seeing that this particular one is on rabbits, maybe I should mention our own rabbit – Benny Buck. It's getting very near to the time for you to be deciding who would like to look after him for the holidays. As you know, it is our class's turn to be responsible for him again. And what I would like to do is for one of you to take him home a

9

few days before we break up. Then – if by some chance – looking after him didn't quite work out, someone else could have a go instead."

The room was alive with excitement. Benny Buck was a favourite subject. Arms were shooting up like rockets. Cries of "Me", "No – *me* ...", "I'm the best one ...", "I *care* ...", "You said your mum was *allergic* to fur ...", "The droppings are good for the garden ..." cascaded in stars of enthusiasm round Miss Broom's tireless ears.

"We took him once before," babbled the twins. "It's only right that he should always go to the place where he's best looked after – which is *our* house. Mr Badger said he'd never seen him looking so good as when *we* looked after him. Our Mam's going to write a special letter to Mr Badger asking if we can *always* look after him, instead of having to fuss round looking for different people all the time. Please Miss Broom, will you promise that if it goes to someone who can't look after it properly, you'll let us have it again?" Their eyes were bulging with purple passion.

"I'll put your names on my list of reserves," Miss Broom smiled tactfully. "But try and remember all the others who want to show that they are kind and good to pets, too."

The twins subsided. It was obvious to them who wanted to get Benny Buck this time. They scowled at Jonny Briggs and he gave them a cool, icy stare.

His heart was thumping indignantly. Surely Miss Broom's memory wasn't *that* bad? The twins had twisted Mr Badger's words! He'd described Benny as *a poor bunny – as good as a Prize Fighter with all those scratches*! And he'd told the whole school that the poor little soul must *never* be allowed to fall out of any more kitchen windows on to gooseberry bushes ... *Good*? ... *kind*? Jonny gulped in anger.

On the way home from school that afternoon, Jonny said to Pam: "Thank goodness that lot's over, and thank goodness Miss Broom allowed me to take the rabbit book home to look at. And thanks a million goodnesses there might be a chance of me looking after Benny Buck. Just imagine a *Briggs* doing that." His face shone with sudden pleasure.

But Pam looked gloomy. She twisted a strand of her shining brown hair from its blue butterfly clip: "Sometimes you're much luckier than me, Jonny. Mum said 'never again' to pets when our Stew's white mice escaped and made a nest in a packet of vacuum-cleaner bags. Anyway, I hope the twins don't get him. Your mum and dad must be really nice, sometimes, letting you look after him."

Jonny went a bit quiet, and they both stood and watched a pigeon eating the remains of a cream cake that had met with an accident on the pavement: "The thing is – I haven't asked them yet," he muttered.

Pam's eyes widened knowingly: "Then Miss Broom'll never let you have it. You've got to bring a signed letter from home saying they'll agree to it. But good luck all the same." She smiled at him and took a crumpled sweet bag from her pocket. She carefully pulled apart two fluffy mint humbugs and gave him one. They spent the next couple of minutes pushing them all over their mouths and gums; pretending to have gum-boils and making strange lumpy faces which dribbled with sticky brown stains. Then they waved each other goodbye.

But as Jonny walked home he just couldn't help wondering what mam and dad would say about the school rabbit. Mrs Prince across the road always called *their* pet rabbits "black and white guzzling furry monsters ..." Ah well ... wait and see ... that was all he could do.

He smiled joyfully as he saw Razzle waiting to greet him at the backyard door. Razzle tried to lick him all over, then they both went to inspect the biscuit tin in the kitchen. They were lucky. There was a packet with a few rich tea biscuits in it. Razzle loved those ....

"Good dog," said Jonny, holding a biscuit high up. "Good dog. Sit ...".

In one quivering breath the biscuit vanished with a flash of shining teeth and pink tongue. Just then Albert's suspicious face loomed up close by. "Don't say you're giving that greedy dog *more* food," he grumbled, peering through his floppy black hair. "It gets better fed than anyone! It's a crime to be feeding *him* on *human* nourishment!"

"It was only *one*, Albert. He never gets Jammy Dodgers or chocolate shortbreads ..."

"And neither do I," said Albert menacingly. "Nobody cares about me in this house. I could starve to death and people would step over me." He began to rummage in the biscuit tin.

Jonny hurried upstairs. There was one solitary biscuit in his pocket. His treasure ... to eat when he was looking at his rabbit book. Please let him be able to have the school rabbit ... please ...

In the bedroom, he put the book on his pillow carefully. His bunk felt warm from the sunshine. He stood and basked in the peace and quiet, gazing round the room with pleasure. The battered old toy box beamed back. The torn comics smiled. And his gold belt sparkled invitingly. There was just time to put it on and be king of a magic world for a quarter of a minute.

Then, zooming back to the ordinary old world of Port Street, he climbed cheerfully up to his bunk to eat his treasure, and look at his book at last. There were lots of pictures in it and loads of pages to read. And the print was nice and big and inviting.

He was just on to page six and reading "How to build your hutches" when his spirits fell ... Albert's shadow was there again.

"What's all this reading lark, then?" enquired Albert with his usual nosiness. He was clutching the empty biscuit packet and as usual crumbs were escaping from his mouth in short bursts of freedom. He walked over to the bunks and put his foot on the bottom rung of the ladder.

"Just a book, Albert. There's nowt about planes in it, or stamps, or ..." Jonny's voice began to fade as Albert lunged almost on top of him and tried to grab it.

"Give it here and stop being so cagey," ordered Albert. "It looks a bit big for you."

In a flash Jonny had managed to wriggle from Albert's octopus-like arms and topple onto the bedroom rug still clutching *Rabbit Care*. "It's a very important *library* book," he panted. "No one's allowed to have it in this house except me – "

But before he could say another word Albert was on the attack again: "Library ... ? You ... ? And why choose those New Zealand ones?"

Jonny looked puzzled: "Not New Zealand. It's rabbits ..." He stepped well out of Albert's way – close to the bedroom door for a quick getaway – and held up the book just enough for Albert to see the picture on the front of it. He might as well let him know a *bit* about it, otherwise Albert would be forever tormenting him.

"Rabbits. That's what I was going to say, twerp!" said Albert witheringly. "New Zealand Whites, that's what they're called. Very big, with white fur and pink eyes. Some people eat them."

Jonny's face dropped a mile. Trust Albert to point that out. "This book's not about eating them," he said defensively. "It's about *caring* for them."

"You have to *care* for them even if you eat them in the end, stupid," said Albert knowledgeably. "You

14

want to give that side of it some serious thought, our Jonny. Rabbit pies could be very popular. I might come in with you on a project like that. It's what's known as enterprise. We could be millionaires ..."

Jonny shook his head. "I just don't want to be, Albert. It's all to do with looking after Benny Buck at school. Miss Broom wants someone to look after him in the holidays and – " Jonny said no more. Albert had completely lost interest.

Swiftly Jonny moved back downstairs with his precious book. Where on earth could he keep it safe? He began to think of all sorts of unsuitable places like behind the sewing machine, and under the chair cushions – until suddenly he found himself staring straight at the small wooden bookshelf where dad kept his *Big Book of Joinery* and mam kept her *Cooking For All*. There wasn't much else on that shelf except a packet of candles in case the electricity ever went off and a pair of Pussy Cat book-ends with the tails broken off.

Without more ado, he stood on a chair and pushed *Rabbit Care* in between *Joinery* and *Cooking*. It looked great!

And it lay there unnoticed for about ten seconds.

"What's that up there?" said his oldest brother, Humph, going to peer at the title on the way to getting the tomato sauce bottle to put on the table for tea.

As quickly as he could, Jonny began to explain. Humph was the only one who ever seemed to listen properly. Mam was still out of the way in the kitchen. She'd just got in from work and was cooking tinned spaghetti and proper chips and beefburgers. Jonny could see her through the open kitchen door as she put out a special plate for Rita with one lettuce leaf, a spoonful of cottage cheese and slice of apple. He checked to see she wasn't frowning or accidentally getting hot fat on her fingers. He wanted it all to be peaceful ...

"A rabbit, eh?" said Humph with a bit of a smile as they both finished setting the table. "You're getting well-prepared with that great encyclopaedia!"

"It's good, though, Humph. It tells you everything about rabbits. And I'll need plenty of time to make a really big rabbit hutch – " He stopped dead as mam came hurrying into the room, but it was too late.

Mam fixed him with a piercing, dagger-like look and Jonny's hand quivered slightly against the knives and forks.

"Surely I didn't hear the word RABBIT HUTCH?" she said accusingly. "Surely no one is hinting at the presence of a RABBIT around this place?" In sudden panic Jonny looked across to the shelf. And mam looked too ... "*Rabbit Care?*" she shouted. "I just don't believe it! Is somebody trying to torture me?"

There was an uneasy silence. No one dared say a word. There was a legend in the house that once, in the dim past, mam got into a *real* temper and a plate of mushy peas got stuck to the ceiling.

"How on earth can anyone imagine that dogs and rabbits mix?" she asked, with a ring of desperation in her voice. "Razzle, and a great dollop of a rabbit, cramped in the same backyard ... is everyone going mad? Dad and I spend our time trying to find more *space* for things, and all the time you lot are filling it with rubbish!"

"Rabbits aren't *rubbish*, mam," said Jonny, in a very small voice.

She turned and glared at him: "I might have known it was you, our Jonny."

"It's the *school* rabbit, mam. You'd like it ... go on, mam ..." he looked at her appealingly. "Be a sport, our mam ..."

"No way is one of those crossing this threshold," she snapped. But the rest of her speech was drowned by Albert crashing into the room like a carthorse.

"Come on then!" said Albert. "Where's the nosh? I'm starving. I've got to be out in three minutes." He stared at the beefburgers and gasped: "Don't say you've gone and got the shrinking ones again!"

"Eat it and shut up! You could do a lot worse. Think yourself lucky," said Humph quietly.

It was one of those meals that disappeared into stomachs in ten giant gulps. But no sooner had mam seen them all gobble it down and dash off out again, than in walked Rita.

"You look a bit tired, love," said mam sympathetically as she trailed to and fro with Rita's Healthy Life meal from the kitchen.

Rita wiped her brow with dramatic weariness and flung down her bag of school books with such force that the sideboard rattled. "I'll kill that Miss Bollinger," she groaned. "She made me stay and clear some mousy-smelling cupboards full of pink blotting paper and arithmetic books from the year dot!"

Rita sat and gazed disparagingly at her lettuce leaf. "What's this then, mam? Is it a meal for a *snail*?"

Mam stared at her weakly. Her brain was always in a bit of a daze where Rita was concerned: "It's what you've got written down on your card in the kitchen drawer, love. I'm only trying to give you exactly what you want. No one can ever accuse me of not trying …"

Rita's nose tilted skyward with dignified scorn: "Look mam – these things may be all right in the middle of summer in a blazingly hot, sunny place. But not *here* at this time of the year."

Mam began to scowl: "I'm not a mind reader, Rita! It's your own Golden Gates Californian Diet Plan …"

"Forget it, mam. That was a century ago! My new Muscular Mountain Plan allows me French fries twice a week and as much steak and kidney pudding as I can eat." Her eyes began to sparkle: "Mavis and I have met these two weight-lifters. Mine says I've got a very good set of biceps and not to starve them too much, so baked beans'll do me tonight till you've got yourself properly organised." Her gaze suddenly

18

drifted towards the bookshelf: "*Rabbit Care*? Who's brought that in?" she began to smoulder with curiosity. But by now mam was in no fit state for further conversation on *anything* as she almost threw the tin opener at Rita from the kitchen drawer. "If you want beans, you know what to do. So just let me and your poor dad have a bit of hush for the rest of the evening. Right?"

Rita's nostrils narrowed in a deep intake of air. She gave her mother a silent puzzled stare. What was up with *her* then? She finished her tea quickly and didn't bother with the tin opener.

Later that evening when mam and dad were finally on their own, dad said casually: "Quite a posh book that one on our shelf. Summat to do with rabbits from the look of it. Used to like rabbits when I was a lad."

"Well, you aren't a lad now, so just you remember," said mam tartly. "Believe me I'll be very glad to see that book vanish from our shelf before any damage is done."

"Damage? Whatever do you mean love?"

"Damage – like hutches being made, and awful upheavals in our backyard."

"Oh ... *that* ... " said dad, a bit sheepishly.

"Yes ... *that* ... " said mam firmly. "So don't you be led astray by our Jonny."

"As if I would ... " laughed dad as they went upstairs to bed. "As if I would ... "

# 2
# The Swap-Over

Next morning at school, Miss Broom was talking about her favourite subject. Jonny Briggs and the whole class knew what *that* was ... It was TREES.

"I want our class to make lots of money for the 'Helping-to-Grow-Trees Fund'," she said.

Everyone looked a bit gloomy. First, because they hadn't even got any money for themselves and second, because it was a bit early in the morning to think about trees.

Quickly, Miss Broom steered the conversation to plans of how it was to work out. "We will make the money by selling home-made cakes and biscuits on our stall at the School Fayre next Saturday," she said. "And by the time you've had your first cookery lesson, today, you should all be expert cooks. We are going to make gingerbread men. Then you can each take one home and perhaps your parents will let you make some more to sell at the Fayre. We must make it a real family effort."

Jonny lifted the lid of his desk very slightly, just to make sure Humph's old woodwork apron was safe for the cookery lesson. Mam had written, *J. Briggs COOKERY* on it in tiny writing with a special marking pen.

The cookery area was one of the old dinner huts divided into two. There was lots of space and the smooth wooden tables gave you plenty of room.

Jonny was really excited as they all stood behind the tables and began to put on their aprons. He'd brought his gold belt to keep his apron tucked up round his waist properly.

"I'm giving you all five currants each," said Miss Broom. "Look after them, as there aren't any more. They are for the eyes and buttons of your gingerbread men."

"Just look at *him* in that great white nighty and stupid old gold belt," muttered Josie to Jinny as they rolled out their dough. "He's only wearing that belt because Miss Broom's lost her glasses. She never even saw he'd got *six* currants instead of five either –"

Jinny nodded and wiped her nose on the back of her hand: "It's ever since he did those magic tricks in the concert." Then she said: "His gingerbread man'll be TERRIBLE. Just you see!"

But Jonny and Pam were too busy to bother about what the twins were saying. "Just cut round it, Jonny – like mine," urged Pam. "And how did you manage to get *six* currants?"

"It was on the floor," whispered Jonny in triumph. "Mine's going to have an extra button!"

"On the *floor*?" gasped Lily Spencer in horror. "It'll be covered with *germs*!"

"It wasn't quite on the floor . . . it fell on a shoe. An' they'll get killed by the cooking." Jonny began to feel quite uncomfortable. It was worse than being in the kitchen at home with his sister Sandra.

"Is it that *bottom* button on your gingerbread man?" asked Pam, anxiously.

He nodded warily. It looked perfect with an extra currant. "Whose shoe was the currant on?" prodded Pam.

Jonny didn't answer, but suddenly he pulled off the extra currant and put it on the table edge. He knew that the shoe it came off was one of a pair that were usually caked with mud from all over the place.

It was at this minute that one of the Brown brothers came sauntering past their end of the table and in a flash the extra currant had gone . . .

"Stop work, a moment," called Miss Broom. "Have you all finished your first gingerbread man?"

"Please Miss Broom, *we* finished ages ago," called Jinny. " . . . *AND* –" she made her eyes stretch almost to the ceiling – "Jonny Briggs got *six* currants instead of five. Why's he always got to be different, miss?"

"I never have!" protested Jonny, secretly thankful that the Browns liked currants even more than he did.

He'd purposely tried to avoid trouble by staying with all his best-behaved friends, and now this! It was crucial for Miss Broom to see that he was one of the most sensible, well-behaved people in the whole class. *Those* were the sort of people she wanted to look after Benny Buck ...

"Trouble makers! Baked Potaters!" sang Pam softly as she pulled her worst monster face at the twins: "He's got five. So shut up."

"Hands up anyone who *hasn't* got a gingerbread man with *two* currant eyes, and three currant buttons," sighed Miss Broom. Heads swizzled in all directions. But no hands went up. Miss Broom gave a sudden dazzling smile. "Excellent!" she said.

"I'm glad Miss Broom's in a good temper again," whispered Jonny. "An' I hope I get the rabbit ... " He began to dream as they stood there, waiting for the gingerbread men to be put in the oven. For, even now, Benny Buck was still in his thoughts.

"What did they say at home about it?" whispered Pam.

"I'm not quite sure ... " Jonny screwed up his eyes a bit and took a deep breath: "Mam knows about it though ... "

Then he said: "Just imagine if the twins did get Benny Buck again," and shuddered. Then they got ready to leave the cookery hut.

23

"Mrs Tallow will take the biscuits out of the oven," said Miss Broom. (Mrs Tallow was the school cook.) "And when you collect them at home-time this afternoon, what do you have to remember?"

"We've-to-remember-to-tell-our-mams-and-dads-to-bake-things-for-the-School-Fayre-and-we've-got-to-show-them-how-to-make – GINGERBREAD MEN!" called Martin Canebender triumphantly in one long breath.

"Doing the cookery was great, wasn't it?" said Jonny to Pam as they hurried to collect their results at the end of the afternoon. In his mind's eye he could already see his very own golden-brown gingerbread man with one slight dimple in its stomach where he'd pulled out the extra currant.

"We'll know which are ours, because mine has a dimple and yours has long legs and big feet." They began to laugh.

But when they arrived at the tables where all the gingerbread men were spread out, their faces changed and they began to look decidedly suspicious. For a start, the biscuits looked ... well ... not quite as wonderful as they'd imagined. Some looked positively gruesome, with cracks and curled-up bits and two of them were regular Burnt Offerings.

Mrs Tallow was very apologetic. "I'm terribly sorry about the two cindery-looking ones," she said. "But there was a bit of trouble with the heat regulator on one of the ovens."

As soon as she said that, there was a sudden closing

24

in round the tables as the orderly queue broke up and everyone pushed forward to claim what they thought a good gingerbread man *should* look like, rather than what most of them *did* look like. And in seconds there were agonised cries as one or two were accidentally broken by impatient grabbers and two were eaten on the spot and three more were found with alien teeth marks in them, said by the Brown brothers to have been made by beings from outer space ...

Jonny and Pam stared in dismay as they were jostled in a sea of moving elbows.

"Arrominter Merryweather's definitely grabbed yours, Jonny," muttered Pam angrily. "And Jinny's grabbed mine!"

But before they could say "Fisherman's Garters", they were stranded like two fish themselves, gasping at the two cindery-looking offerings.

"Serves you both right," chortled Josie. "We knew yours'd be the worst of the lot."

Jonny's fists began to clench and unclench, as he stared at the two awful biscuits lying there. How could he possibly take one of those home? He'd be the laughing stock of their house! And as for mam or anyone else helping him based on *that* ... "It wouldn't surprise me," he thought miserably, "if our mam decided to come to school and tell Mr Badger that we were wasting our time bringing rubbish like that home ... " And that wouldn't give Jonny much hope over other important things ... like school rabbits for instance ...

And then – like a sudden ray of sunshine from heaven – he became aware of Mrs Tallow's beaming face. "Whatever is she smiling for?" he thought grumpily.

"I knew those two would be left," said Mrs Tallow as she uncovered two cardboard plates hidden by a large linen tea-towel. "Who are the two children who are left without?"

All eyes turned on Jonny Briggs and Pam. "These are for you two, then," smiled Mrs Tallow "You can keep the plates."

Everyone gasped in surprise and even envy as Jonny and Pam were presented with two very large, perfectly-made gingerbread men with big cherries for buttons. The only ones with cherries ...

"Please, Mrs Tallow," called Jinny quickly: "There's been a mistake. Those burnt ones belonged to me and my sister. We must have got theirs. They can have them back if they want ... "

But this time they were too late. Jonny and Pam had thanked Mrs Tallow and were off home across the grey school yard with their unexpected rewards like a couple of rockets.

"Good luck at last!" yelled Jonny. Then he calmed down a bit because they were getting near the main road. "All the same I don't suppose our mam will let me show *her* how to make things. And the last time our Sandra made toffee she left it to cool by the back door and our dad put his foot in it ... "

"Won't they even let you make that cold coconut

fudge with condensed milk?" asked Pam anxiously.

"Not a hope . . . " Then Jonny added: "If it was just dad and me without the others . . . he *might* . . . if there was no football on."

"Ours is all right as long as his car hasn't conked out," said Pam thoughtfully. Then she smiled: "Maybe this time it'll all be different. Especially when they see our *Ace* gingerbread men! Aren't they fantastic? The only ones with cherries!"

"Fantastico . . . marvellous-o . . . vunderbar!" added Jonny, cheering up at last as they parted for their separate homes. "See you . . . "

Jonny could already hear Albert clattering about upstairs the minute he opened the door into the hall. Albert was trying to do three things at once. He was trying to revive a balsa-wood glider that had all the tissue paper torn off its frame, eat Pot Noodles, and play a mouth-organ for when he started up his pop group The Tigers again.

"I'm off out in two minutes," he said to Jonny warningly, "so don't you dare touch that plane whilst I'm away . . . "

Jonny nodded silently. He always agreed promptly to any plan which involved Albert vanishing quickly to torment someone else in another house.

Tea-time was almost perfect as Jonny produced the wonderful gingerbread man with the special cherry buttons.

"And do you mean to say you actually made *that yourself*, luvvy?" said mam, putting it on a special, lacy-edged plate and staring at it reverently.

"Nearly ... " Jonny began to mumble shyly. "Pam Dean and me got a sort of extra reward for ours, from Mrs Tallow the cook."

Mam shook her head slowly in astounded and happy disbelief, and a huge balloon began to swell up in her mind showing Chef Jonathan Briggs (Cordon Bleu, red and sky-blue-pink ... the best letters after your name in the whole of world cookery) being honoured yet again with the Mrs Beeton Golden Biscuit Trophy and a trip to some island paradise for the whole of the Briggs family – on Concorde. Then – to Jonny's delight – she gave him a swift peck of a kiss as she put a jar of piccalilli on the table.

"It seems too nice to break into, doesn't it?" she said to dad as she still gazed at the gingerbread man. "Cherries and all. Isn't it wonderful what they can do these days?"

Dad looked up slightly from the *Gazette*. "Mmm. Wonderful, love. Oh aye ... excellent. Very nice." Then he gave a slight groan and said: "Eeh, but I hope the Boro' gets out of the doldrums."

Everyone seemed in such a good temper as they munched away that Jonny decided to broach the subject of the School Fayre, and making more stuff at home for it.

"They want us to show *you* how to bake and all, mam ... gingerbread men ... " His face fell as he saw Rita suddenly sparkle with interest.

"Show *us* how to make them?" whooped Rita, "Of

28

all the cheek! It's typical of that place."

Rita really began to get into her stride. She was quite good at long speeches at meal times because, until now, her lettuce and tomato snacks enabled her to keep her mouth pretty empty and ready for talking. And if the rest of the family had theirs stuffed full, it was hard for them to answer back quickly enough.

Rita turned pleadingly to her mother and stuck out her elbow towards Jonny like a signpost: "Can you imagine what it would be like, mam — if *he* got going? Flour and water everywhere and him going mad with a rolling-pin? And just when you've spent all that time painting the cupboards!"

But for once, mam wasn't being quite as swayed: "Fair do's Rita. He's not had quite the same encouragement in the kitchen as you girls. Our Jonny might be a chef one day — if he was interested."

Jonny gave a gasp of alarm: "But I don't want to be a chef, mam. I want to play for the Boro'."

"Quite right lad," said dad, looking up and winking. "They could do with a few more good players!"

"But I'd like to make some more of those gingerbread men for our class's stall at the School Fayre ... Go, on mam ... *Please?*"

"Don't you dare, mother!" Rita's voice sounded off like a pistol shot. "Mavis is coming round. We'll need this table *and* that one in the kitchen."

"What on earth for, Rita?" Mam began to look harassed and a big frown appeared across her eyebrows.

"Mavis and I are trying out these new hair styles tonight ... "

"Hay-stack styles more like," whispered Jonny under his breath.

"Shut up – you," snapped Rita. "We'll be doing a bit of shading and toning, too. *Right here* –please note. It's no good being upstairs in the bathroom because as sure as eggs are eggs there'd be a long queue wanting to interrupt."

Jonny gazed pleadingly at his mam: "Don't let her have the table down here, our mam. She always gets everything! Miss Broom wants us to make the biscuits as soon as possible. Pam and me wants to take ours in tomorrow. Be a sport, mam ... "

It was all growing into a real tussle and no way was Rita going to be outdone: "I'm warning you for the last time, mother, if you let him loose in our kitchen you'll rue the day!" She looked at her watch: "I'm off to Mavis's now – but we'll be back here double quick. And we don't want *him* around."

She flounced out with such a swirl that the strong current of air ruffled dad's paper. "Has she gone?" he groaned. "A little bit of peace is all I ask for."

Mam turned to Jonny: "Look pet – how's this for an idea? I've got to go out in a minute to our Marilyn's but before I go I'll make you a batch of those gingerbread men for school. I'll pop them in the oven and you can wash up the things whilst I'm out." She stared at his face: "No need to look all *sulky*. You said your teacher wanted us to take part."

Jonny tried to look more cheerful. He was always having to explain school: "They didn't want you to do it *all*, mam. Miss Broom meant us all to get together and ... me and all ... " He brightened: "Even dad could try."

But his mother wasn't listening. She was already busy getting the mixing bowl, flour, fat, sugar and ginger and making a dough. He watched miserably as she cheerfully mixed it and rolled it out and made a batch of gingerbread men in the twinkling of an eye.

"It's ages since I made these. Get the baking trays and help me put them on – there's a good boy. It's time I was going."

When she'd gone, Jonny began to cool down. At least he'd have some biscuits – even if she had made them all. And they smelt delicious – it made everything seem warm and extra homely. She'd left him in charge of watching for the right time to get them out of the oven, too. It was better than nothing. And that time had arrived just as Albert came bursting through the door.

"Phew," Albert breathed deeply. "Summat smells good! I'm starving. There was this kid at Billy's house and he's worked out an infallible gambling system for the football pools. Where's our dad? I must tell him about it."

"He's talking to a man from the Residents' Association in the front-room about job shortages. Do us a favour Albert, get the biscuits out of the oven for us ... "

31

For once, Albert actually did what Jonny told him – without even an argument – and helped him put them out on a wire tray on the living-room table.

"We're not allowed to eat any," said Jonny. "Mam made them specially for me to take to school."

Albert's face dropped: "School? What a waste!" Then a crafty Albert-look crept across his face and he said: "But you'll need to taste 'em. The best food always has to be tasted. Some people get *paid* just for tasting food and drinks to make sure they're O.K. Supposing there's too much salt in them or summat? I'll test 'em for you when I've been upstairs. They should've cooled off by then."

As Albert leapt away, Jonny stood there thinking. He could see by Albert's greedy eyes that *Protection of Biscuits* was the name of the game. Albert was quite capable of testing every biscuit into complete nothingness.

Jonny moved swiftly into the kitchen and looked round – then hastily he popped the trays on top of the small wire vegetable rack near the washing machine and draped a clean tea-towel round them. He was back in the living-room only seconds before Albert.

"Where've they gone?" gasped Albert.

Jonny tried not to answer: "Where have what gone ... ?" he muttered.

"Come on. Don't try acting giddy goats. Those biscuits. Where are they?"

"Did you tell dad about that boy who's going to win the pools?"

"Don't try *that* on. Where are they?" Albert grabbed Jonny's arm: "Where've you hidden them? I'm *trying* to do you a favour if you did but know it ... "

"Ow! Gerroff! They're for school," yelped Jonny. "Our mam made them. She'll be mad if they get eaten. Leave go my arm!"

Albert let go, just as Humph came in: "Something cooking?" asked Humph.

"In more ways than one," said Albert. "Something *was* cooking but he's hidden them."

"They aren't *mine*," said Jonny. "It's something special. Those biscuits are for school." Jonny explained what had happened.

Humph looked at Albert: "It's no good, Alby. It's just no good wanting to test them. People'll find out soon enough if they don't taste right without us getting mixed up in it."

"What a house!" roared Albert in disgust. "If Arnold Watson pops across with that magazine tell him I've gone to the chippy!" And he rushed out, leaving all the doors open.

"Where did you hide them then?" asked Humph a bit later. "Will they have cooled off enough to put them away properly?"

"They're covered in a tea-towel just by the washing machine on that wire vegetable rack ... "

Eagerly Jonny rushed to get them. And as he did – his eyes met a *dreadful* sight. Dreadful for some, and absolute *paradise* for others ... like small, hungry, energetic dogs with names like ... Razzle ...

Razzle looked up at Jonny and wagged his tail and licked his chops. There were just one or two biscuit crumbs left on the floor to be finished off before the vanishing act was complete. Jonny and Humph looked at each other in startled silence.

# 3
# Secret Plan

Jonny was close to tears. No hope of a single biscuit for school now, and the prospect of mam coming home and raising the roof when she heard what had happened to *her* efficiently-made gingerbread men...

"Cheer up! There's worse happens at sea." Humph put his arms round Jonny's shoulders just as dad appeared.

"Is there a funeral going on?" asked dad.

"Razzle's just had a very big meal," said Humph, trying to keep the disappointment out of his voice.

Jonny brushed a hand across his face: "Mam'll go mad."

"Couldn't we make some more?" said Humph, looking at dad.

Dad eyed him with sudden sharpness: "Who? Your mam's out – "

"Us make 'em," urged Humph. "Jonny knows how. He just said … You and all, dad? While the coast's clear. Just the three of us."

Dad took a deep breath: "Let's get my slippers on first then," he said grudgingly. "If I've got to labour over a bit of cookery I might as well do it in comfort."

No sooner said than done. Jonny's heart began to soar again as they tucked tea-towels round their waists and got cracking. The living-room was awash with flour as a new batch of gingerbread men began to be spread on baking trays in all directions.

"I must admit I quite enjoyed that lot," said dad when, red-faced and smiling, he saw the last tray disappear into the oven. "I reckon we should be in the Guinness Book of Records for the speed of that little operation … And now – if you don't mind, I'll go and get washed and brushed up before mam gets back."

Jonny and Humph tore round the living-room in a frenzy. "Get the sweeper for the floor, quick!" said Humph. "Wipe the grease off the door handle and shake the ends of the curtains."

It was like a sort of obstacle race as they hurried about with shovels and brushes and pushed all the washing-up into the sink. "Only another five minutes left of guaranteed safety," breathed Humph. "Three minutes for the washing-up and two to get the biscuits out of the oven and on to the wire trays!"

Sweat was beginning to appear on their noses as they finally brought everything back to normal again. And not a second too soon because Mavis and Rita came strolling in. Jonny was on his own now to face them. He stared at them innocently.

"What a lovely smell, Rita ... " said Mavis appreciatively. "Real home cooking . . . like Granny's. We'll be able to have more of that now we're boosting our muscles."

But Rita scowled primly and said: "I'm not sure that we shall Mavis. *You* carry a lot of surplus fat, you know. It's *muscle* that we want. Plenty of protein ... that's the answer."

Mavis began to peer at the gingerbread men on the wire trays with close interest: "Are they Animal Crackers?" she asked timidly.

Rita looked puzzled and came to give them her official verdict. She halted suspiciously: "Not *quite*, Mavis. More a case of gingerbread men gone crackers if you ask me. Funny, that ... our mam usually does them really well. And she uses the pastry cutter. These look a real higgledy-piggledy hotch-potch."

Then she sniffed and said: "Ah well, she's getting very old now – poor soul. She's probably past it."

They were just launching into a long-winded conversation about how old certain pop stars were and what an awful fate it must be to reach forty, when in came mam herself. And at this point Rita and Mavis decided not to do toning and hair shading but to go back to Mavis's to try on wire bracelets, instead.

(They spent half their lives walking backwards and forwards as they yapped away.)

At first mam drew the same deep breaths as everyone else when the warm scents of baking crept to her nose. Then she looked at the results lying there so proudly. "Are those the ... biscuits?" she almost stammered the words.

"Yes, mam," said Jonny nervously. "They're smashing, aren't they."

"I'm not so sure about that ... " She just couldn't get over how wobbly they looked; like some huge ungainly family, some fat, some thin, some small, some tall; some with eyes at the very tops of their heads, and some with mouths where their noses should have been. And yet she distinctly remembered making them all exactly the same with the biscuit cutter ...

Her thoughts were interrupted as dad walked in carrying a large, empty, biscuit tin. She'd never seen him carrying that tin before in all their married life!

"Just going to pop them in it love," he said cheerfully: "get 'em away to safety ... "

Hastily he and Jonny began putting them into the tin. "Careful," muttered dad. "We don't want any broken ... It took us a long time to – "

Mam looked at him sharply: "Took *you* a long time? You never make biscuits! You wouldn't know how to start – "

"True, love – true," said dad hastily. "You've got a point."

38

"On the other hand," mam's eyes began to focus on the tin like a powerful magnet: "They did look a bit funny compared to how they usually turn out ... I'll just have another look – "

Jonny grasped the last gingerbread man firmly, and in seconds they were resting in their new home with the lid tightly fastened.

"I'll take 'em away for you son," said dad, giving him a sly wink. "I'll put them on the top shelf till morning. We wouldn't like Razzle to get them or anything would we? We've all done very well. Hop along to bed now, there's a good lad."

Jonny didn't need telling twice. The sooner the biscuits were forgotten the better. Rabbits seemed a safer subject.

"I'll just get my rabbit book to read for a bit, then," he said as he took it from the shelf.

When he'd gone mam said: "He's got rabbit-mania at the moment. It's absolutely ridiculous, him wanting to look after that school one."

"Stop worrying, love. It may never happen," dad smiled and looked quite dreamy: "I once had a very nice floppy-eared one when I was a nipper. But it escaped and was never seen again."

"That's exactly the sort of palaver we'll have, and it's *not going to happen*," declared mam firmly.

The door slammed and a regal voice suddenly broke the few moments of discussion. "What escaped and was never seen again?" asked Rita who'd arrived back home. Then, like sudden mental telepathy, she said: "Not that *rabbit*? It's absolute cruelty to keep them penned up in piffling little hutches in backyards."

"I couldn't agree more, our Rita," said mam.

"The hutch wouldn't be *that* small," said dad, suddenly showing his colours: "I could rustle up a pretty large one. And it could always come out for a run round for a bit of exercise ... "

"Presumably when *Razzle* is elsewhere?" suggested Rita, with a majestic tone in her voice. Then she said: "Get us a gingerbread, mam. Just to test 'em ... I'm quite peckish."

"Of course you are, love. You're a growing girl. I'm glad you've gone off all those silly lettuce leaves," cooed mam encouragingly. "Fetch us the tin, dad."

Dad suddenly went all washed-out-looking. "It's a bit late for rich things like that, lass."

"Whatever's come over you, dad?" gasped mam.

With deep dread, dad went to the shelf and reluctantly brought back the tin. Rita took one quick horrified look inside: "These aren't your biscuits mam, I'm ready to swear it! Mavis and I saw them on the wire trays, and I wasn't sure then. But now I'm certain! What's been going on? These have been made by a whole load of bungling idiots. Just look at the *shapes*! Surely you didn't let our Jonny make any? I warned you and warned you ... "

Dad vanished like a sudden shadow. But this time Rita had overstepped the mark. Mam was feeling tired. Quite frankly she didn't care now who'd made the wretched biscuits: "For heaven's sake SHUT UP Rita! I couldn't care less at present. Get that one eaten and don't mention them ever again." Her voice cooled down as Jonny appeared in his pyjamas carrying the rabbit book.

"I'll just put it back on the shelf, mam." Jonny suddenly froze as he saw Rita with the biscuit tin, and far from shutting up – she was off on another tack: "Chuck them away, mam. They're a load of rubbish. You can't send those mis-shapen things to the School Fayre. Give them to Razzle."

Like a sudden spark of lightning Jonny sprang across the room and tried to grab the tin from her: "They're *mine*. Get off them – YOU! They're special. *Dad* and me made those. Our dad and Humph and me."

"You three?" Mam looked completely flabbergasted. "Stop clutching that tin, Rita," she said. "Open the lid and let me have another look." She gazed at the miraculous jumble. "This is the first time your dad has ever made a biscuit, let alone an actual gingerbread man in the whole of his life!" She opened and shut her mouth speechlessly. "It's like a sort of milestone in our lives. A piece of Briggs' family history. It just shows that even the people you think you know best in all the world can rise to – *making biscuits*!"

Rita whispered: "It must have been like climbing Everest for him, our mam." Then she added drily: "Do you think we ought to frame one?"

When dad came back into the room they were all still staring at the tin in subdued silence.

"If you've all quite finished the post-mortem," he grunted, "Jonny and I will put them back on the shelf in the kitchen."

When they were in the kitchen, he said: "I'm putting the tin right there next to that old yellow tin where I keep my cabbage seeds and vegetable labels – so don't go and take the wrong one, will you, son? I reckon we can't stand too much of what happened tonight."

Jonny nodded happily and smiled. At last it had all worked out safely. At least he could go to bed knowing that his precious cooking was safely packed away and waiting for school tomorrow. Thank goodness.

"Goodnight, dad."

"Goodnight, our Jonny. Sleep tight."

# 4
# Suspects

Jonny slept like a log, and although he intended to get up extra early the next morning he was a bit late. But he didn't worry because he knew everything was well organised. All he had to do was to get his breakfast and then collect the tin from the shelf.

It was a lovely sunny morning. Outside in the yard the sparrows were all twittering away on wash-house roofs, and high in the sky were a few sea-gulls. Jonny was all set. He said goodbye to Razzle. Then he hurried back to the kitchen to collect his biscuit tin.

But – to his utter amazement – even though he hunted round every place he could think of – it had completely vanished!

When Jonny told Pam about it at school her eyes

went as round as saucers. "Whatever can have happened? Do you think the Port Street ghost has come back?"

"I'll nip back home at dinner-time, just to check up again," he said. Then he added: "I wish our house was normal like everyone else's. Nothing ever seems to turn out the way you expect."

"Hurry up you two!" shouted Mr Hobbs who was on playground duty. He was tugging hard at his grey-and-black pullover and scowling a bit because he knew it had shrunk. "Straighten yourselves up and walk in line with the others properly!"

"I wish Miss Broom didn't seem to like him so much ..." whispered Pam under her breath, as they all filed in to school.

At dinner-time, Jonny finally decided to ask Miss Broom if he could call back home for his biscuit tin. She was quite pleasant about it: "Don't be long," she said, "but make sure you get your dinner first."

"What's up?" said Humph, when he saw Jonny arriving back. Humph was sitting peacefully on his own at the living-room table in his school clothes playing chess and eating chips out of a newspaper.

"Have a chip, but don't eat the lot," he said.

"I couldn't find the biscuits this morning," Jonny explained. "All our class had brought stuff for the Fayre except me, and the twins said I couldn't make a proper biscuit if I tried till Domesday." He hesitated: "Do you think it's that ghost?" he asked in a sort of small voice.

Humph shook his head: "There's sure to be a logical explanation." He led Jonny cheerfully into the kitchen. "Let's have another look. You probably didn't have enough time this morning."

Then he asked Jonny if he'd had his dinner.

"A bit. But I hadn't time for seconds ... "

"Get yourself some bread from the bread bin, make yourself a cheese sarni, and get a drink of milk."

Jonny went to the bread bin and as he lifted the lid he saw a large brown paper bag almost covering the sliced loaf next to it. It was full of the GINGER-BREAD MEN!

"Someone's obviously dumped them in there and used that tin for something else," said Humph. "Just what you might have expected."

"Thanks Humph," said Jonny as he got ready to rush back to school. "If it hadn't been for you telling me to make a cheese sarni – I'd never have known!"

When Jonny produced his biscuits at school the twins were rather disappointed. "*Amazing*," they said. "But please, Miss Broom – don't you think they look a bit – well a bit ... ?" they both began to giggle.

"They look extremely tempting and original," answered Miss Broom giving the twins a stern look. "The Briggs family have done us proud."

"Our dad made most of 'em," said Jonny with delight.

The twins subsided. There was an unbroken rule in life. If a *dad* was involved, nothing more could be said.

The Saturday of the School Fayre was another clear bright day, and for once dad had a slight feeling of excitement in his bones as he and mam dutifully trundled to school.

The school hall was packed with a milling crowd of assorted people all weaving their way in and out of awkward spaces full of push-chairs, small children, fat grandads and weighty ladies with big shopping bags.

Mr Badger, the headmaster, in his best navy-blue striped suit kept showing up above a sea of heads with a worried expression on his face then disappearing like a submerging submarine.

Mr Hobbs was running a tombola stall in his usual grey-and-black check pullover.

Mr Box, the caretaker, was in a corner telling the Brown brothers off for making the school pipes wobble more than they should. And Miss Broom was smiling enthusiastically as she manned the Home Baking in Aid of Trees Stall.

"That looks the best stall of all, love," remarked dad, as they shuffled and buffeted their way towards it.

But one person who was completely uninterested in all this was Rita. She was at home with Mavis. "I wouldn't go near that school again if you paid me a million pounds," she said. "But I'm glad the rest of them have cleared off and we've got this place to ourselves for a change. It isn't often our house is completely empty on a Saturday afternoon."

On the living-room table in front of them was the biscuit tin Jonny had hunted for so desperately. It was open and full of small bottles of various tablets. Rita and Mavis began to look at all the bottles in the biscuit tin. "I thought we were supposed to have gone off all these vitamin tablets, Rita. I thought it was pure wholesome food and fresh air again – like granny and grandad believe in."

"What *is* the matter with you this afternoon?" Rita glared at her warningly. "You can't expect Claude to be interested in you – if you aren't interested in what *he* likes ..."

But Mavis stuck to her guns: "I'm not sure whether I like muscle men either. I've been limping all week ever since he accidentally trod on my foot."

Rita softened slightly: "Perhaps we've been doing too much muscle-building all at once, Mavis. Go and turn on the posture music and we'll walk round the room with books on our heads for a bit. Get that big book of *Cookery For All* and Jonny's heavy rabbit book."

With great solemnity they placed the books carefully on top of their heads. Rita made sure that Mavis had the rabbit book because it was apt to be a bit slippery and fall off.

Then, after a few careful and semi-dignified parades past the sideboard and a few surreptitious looks at themselves through the mirror – Rita decided it was time to pack up.

"We'd better scoot before the rabble gets back,"

she announced. "Put the books in your flight bag, Mave. We'll do the next lot of training at your place while your Granny and Grandad are at the Evergreen Club."

As mam, dad and Jonny strolled back from the School Fayre they all agreed it had been a roaring success. "I was right proud of our gingerbread men selling so well," smiled dad.

When they got in, the house was all calm and quietly sunny in the late afternoon. "I'll just put the kettle on," said mam.

"Good idea, love," said dad.

"And I'll just look at my rabbit book," said Jonny, somehow knowing that mam was in such a good mood she wouldn't even mind mention of that fateful word. Then he stopped dead ... it had gone! What was happening? First the biscuit tin and now this! In a quick, low voice he told dad it was missing: "And that tin you put the biscuits in went an' all," he added, "but I never said, in case it caused a fuss."

Dad looked puzzled and frowned slowly.

"What's wrong *now*?" said mam as she brought in the tea.

Dad hesitated. He didn't want to break the peace of a nice afternoon by mentioning mam's most unfavourite subject yet again. "Er ... nothing, love. Just – er – well, it's our Jonny's school library book, it seems to have gone missing off our shelf."

Mam began to simmer with anger. Her eyes sparkled angrily. "And not only *his* book, I notice. *My* big cookery book. WHERE'S THAT? I've never known a home like it for things disappearing. And the very time when I wanted it specially to copy out that recipe for Spiced Date Cake to take round to our Marilyn's tonight."

Mam was so mad she overflowed the cups of tea on to the saucers. "When I find out who's taken those books, there's going to be a *great deal* of trouble." Her mouth had clamped into a hard line.

The rest of Saturday went by, and the rest of Sunday and mam was getting more and more suspicious with everyone. On Monday morning when Albert was the only one except herself in the living-room, she asked about it once more.

"Cookery book?" chuntered Albert miserably. "I've got better things to bother about than cookery books! An' anyway, who wants to read any more? You're out of date, our mam. It's all on video now!"

"All I'm saying is, Albert," said mam as she whisked in and out from the kitchen, "that I hope *you* haven't been up to anything. You don't get much for second-hand cookery books these days you know. And that rabbit book of our Jonny's is a LIBRARY book. If that goes missing you'll have to pay the cost of a new one."

"*I* will?" yelled Albert, beginning to get really rattled. "Why pick on *me*. Don't you believe me or summat when I tell you I've never seen the stupid things? Why should it always be me who's under suspicion? Is it because me hair's too long or summat? I'm treated worse than anyone else in this family – added to which I'm half-starved and this cornflakes packet is completely empty!"

Mam didn't wait to hear any more. She was almost late for work as it was, but she couldn't resist a last parting shot to the effect that she expected the books back by the time she got home at tea-time.

"I'm innocent," roared Albert. "Won't *anybody* believe me?"

The house remained completely silent ...

# 5
# Minders

It was a happy morning at school. The whole of Jonny's class was glowing with quiet pride over the results of the School Fayre.

"The biscuits, sweets and gingerbread men were wonderful," said Miss Broom, beaming at them all. "A bumper amount was made for our school funds, and also for the preservation of our native woodland trees. So now it's time to turn to that other important subject … "

Everyone knew what she was going to say.

"B...E...N...N...Y  B...U...C...K," they chorused.

"We will just go through the procedure for looking after our school rabbit," she said briskly. "Looking after animals is a serious and responsible occupation.

That is why you *must* bring a signed form from your parent or guardian saying that they will allow you to look after the rabbit."

Before she could take another breath, she was flooded out with a welter of signals calculated to catch her attention, more than the usual arm waving, as the air reverberated with: "Please, miss ... ME", and "Shut up YOU – you can't even manage the needs of a garden gnome!" and "I'll do it, miss – we've still got the hutch from the one that died."

And in the foreground of all this enthusiasm were the twins – already out at the front of the class, breathing heavily down Miss Broom's neck and holding out plump and pleading hands for the form to take home for signing.

"Sit down immediately and see me at the end of the morning," said Miss Broom. "The rest of you ... just *calm down* and put your hands up *quietly* if you think you are interested."

She looked at a list of their names and called each one out as she ticked it off as a possible minder. "Jinny and Josie, Lily Spencer, Peter Constable, Halima, Tarek, Ranjeet, Martin Canebender, Jonny Briggs ..."

"JONNY BRIGGS?" Josie's voice exploded like a whistling wombat: "Don't tick him, Miss Broom, he couldn't look after a feather duster!"

The class went very quiet, mainly in case Miss Broom pounced on them – especially if *they* wanted to look after Benny Buck, too.

"He's very good at looking after things," said Pam loyally. "His dog won that prize in our school pet show – so there!"

"Razzle the *guzzle, he'll* need a *muzzle*," chirruped Jinny, who was getting very good at making things rhyme. "It's the sort of dog that'll swallow a rabbit whole, Miss Broom. It's not right to tempt pets to eat each other."

Jonny's face went scarlet. If he'd been in the school yard he would have run the twins to ground and had them pleading for mercy behind the dustbins, but here he was powerless. How *dare* they say things like that about Razzle – the cleverest and best dog in the world?

"Please, Miss Broom," he said slowly, as he tried to retain his dignity and keep his temper, "Razzle wouldn't ever harm anybody – or rabbits – or anything. And I've been learning all about looking after rabbits in the rabbit book from school." It was a long, serious, well-composed reply and he felt quite proud of it. He was calm now and his face had gone back to its ordinary colour.

Miss Broom looked quite pleased: "Good," she said. Then she looked at everyone and said: "I'm pleased that the twins are getting so good at making up rhymes. Perhaps we should all try making one up about our favourite pet. It can have four lines and two of them must rhyme. You can all be doing that whilst I go and have a word with Mr Hobbs about the pipes in the cloakroom."

Jonny grasped his pen firmly. He took a deep breath, and like someone plunging into the cold sea he wrote his rhyme all in one go in case he suddenly sank half-way.

"My dog Razzle is black and white.
He's good and kind and clever.
He stays in his kennel at night when it's dark
And in the day he plays in the park."

"It's really good!" gasped Pam.

He smiled proudly. "Some day I might try writing another one," he said.


"I wish you'd stop flexing your muscles in front of the mirror while we're all eating our teas, Rita," said mam. "Isn't it time you got your homework done instead?"

Dad buried his head in the *Gazette* and lulled himself into the deeper and more serious troubles of the Boro as Rita spun round angrily.

"Look mam – pardon *me* – but I'm quite capable of deciding how to plan my life. Never yet have I failed to do what is required for that sixth-form dump and that awful Miss Bollinger. And for everybody's *personal* information, seeing they're always so nosy – Mavis and I are off to the Sports Centre in a minute to do a spot of weight-lifting with Claud and Felix. And *that* will increase the oxygen flow to our brains and enable *me* to do my HOMEWORK when I get back ... SATISFIED?"

Mam subsided hastily and decided to have a go at Albert instead. She was in one of her niggly moods. "What about my cookery book, Albert? Have you found it yet?"

"Oh yes?" said Albert cynically. "So I'm next for the chopping block am I? You can't boss her about so you decide to get at me about something I know nothing about – "

"My rabbit book's gone an' all – don't forget," chipped in Jonny anxiously.

Albert stuffed the remains of a meat and potato pie into his mouth and stood up hastily: "I'm not staying here to be interrogated like some common criminal. If any of the Tigers call – tell 'em I've escaped to Tommy Fitzpatrick's where nobody nags you."

As Albert rushed out through the front door he happened to let Mavis in. She was carrying her flight bag – bought in case she and Rita were ever whisked away on some glamorous plane trip.

She stood nervously by the door. "Will we need to take the books to put on our heads, Rita? I've brought them back – just in case," she whispered.

"If you're going to talk lass – talk!" said dad bluntly from behind the paper. "I can *ignore* talk. But I just can't abide whispering."

"I was just asking Rita about the BOOKS," said Mavis in a loud voice, going quite pink.

Suddenly Rita was clamped in the piercing stares of two pairs of eyes as mam and Jonny glared at her with dawning truth.

"We haven't time to bother with silly old books just now," muttered Rita hurriedly, as they hustled out.

"Did you see *that*, our mam," howled Jonny. "That's my RABBIT BOOK in that flight bag ... "

"And my COOKERY BOOK ... " said mam bitterly.

Jonny was up in arms: "Anything could happen if she takes them to that Sports Centre. They're not taking them there!" Jonny rushed out of the house shouting at the top of his voice for Rita and Mavis to bring back the books. Mam and dad looked at each other, and groaned.

It was really a waste of time for Jonny to try and struggle against the might of Mavis and Rita when they were on the rampage – arrayed in their war-paint and training as muscle maidens into the bargain. And it showed – Jonny came back home slowly and stubbornly after a rather undignified street tussle in which he had been shoved unmercifully into a very prickly hawthorn bush, told he was a disgrace to the whole of Port Street and informed that he was nothing but an evil-faced little zombie.

Jonny hurried upstairs to the bedroom, wiping a tear-stained face. His hair was spiked and tousled and there was a large smear of blood on his face from a scratch.

Humph was lying on his bed listening to a tape as Jonny related the whole awful saga: " ... An' she said she'd a good mind to leave my rabbit book in the changing rooms of the Sports Centre accidentally on purpose just to teach me a lesson!'' He gulped with sadness and despair.

"How very anti-social," said Humph with calm, concealed rage. "So, if she does that – we'll report her to the chief librarian who happens to be Todger Wentworth's father's brother."

"I'll get my own back," muttered Jonny fiercely. "She's not going to get away with it. Just because I'm younger and smaller – she thinks she can do *anything*. And she CAN'T!''

He rushed straight out of the bedroom in a sudden surge of angry energy and dashed into Rita's sacred boudoir. He was looking round feverishly for the ultimate revenge, but didn't dare to touch things like make-up and talcum powder this time, after that other painful episode ... Then he turned and went downstairs, and walked into the front-room where Rita often left her school books.

Oh yes ... thought Jonny to himself. She keeps her school books well tucked away in safety in here because we don't often use this room. But she doesn't give a fig about other people's books.

Her school case was open. He grabbed the biggest and most important-looking book he could see. It was her Project Homework text-book.

Then he went up to her bedroom, burrowed underneath her matress like a mole and hid the book underneath. He emerged triumphant. A simple and satisfactory retaliation ... !

Rita arrived back from the Sports Centre much earlier than Jonny had imagined. He heard her settling down in the living-room with her books as he waited breathlessly at the top of the stairs. Then he heard Humph – who was also downstairs now – questioning her.

"I hope you aren't going to park yourself there all night," said Rita, ignoring his question. "There's nothing worse than having a big goofy face gawping at you when you're doing an important project."

"It seems," said Humph – completely unperturbed – "that two books are missing from that shelf. One is mam's cookery book, and the other's Jonny's library book. And up to now it's our Albert that's been getting all the flak ... "

"How very sad. Please clear off," said Rita coldly.

"Not before you say where those books are," said Humph, just as coldly.

"Mind your own business," snapped Rita. "It's nothing to do with you, anyway. You always did fancy yourself as the judge and jury. But – if you *must* know – they're in Mavis's flight bag. And at some convenient time for Mavis and me – we shall probably put them back on our shelf. SATISFIED?"

She glared at him and began to rummage through her school case looking more and more perplexed and angry with every second. And then her attention was distracted as mam came in from visiting Marilyn at Hemlington. Mam spent quite a bit of time visiting Marilyn – she was mam's oldest married daughter.

58

Marilyn was a bit lonely at times on the new housing estate and also mam loved new houses with their nice big windows and fitted kitchens.

"I'm afraid I've got a bit of bad news," mam said sadly as she sat down wearily. "Marilyn's puppy has been run over. It ran out of the garden when some children were playing ball – right under the wheels of a van."

There was a heavy silence. No one knew quite what to say.

"The man in the van took it to the Vet's Hospital at Moorcliff House," mam went on, "but it's a toss-up as to whether it'll survive – poor little soul." She took out her handkerchief and quickly dabbed her eyes.

"I'll make you a cup of tea, mam," said Rita suddenly. "It must have been quite a shock."

For a while Rita became quite human, kind and polite, then her hard exterior returned as mam said: "Sandra was at Marilyn's for her tea – so she's staying there overnight because Steve had to go to Nottingham."

"Sandra's getting into a real stay-away," said Rita, a trifle jealously. "What with weekend training courses and always staying with our Marilyn. Anyway it suits me. At least I've got more room in that poky little bedroom to do my exercises." Then she said: "And you'd better get that telly turned off, our dad – because I need it quiet for my homework and there's no light bulb in the other room."

"A better plan," suggested dad drily, as he switched off the television, "would've been for our Rita to go and do her homework at Marilyn's and for our Sandra to be here instead. At least that way we'd get a patch of peace and good cooking all in one go." And shaking his head slightly, he left the room.

"He's just thoroughly *spoilt*," muttered Rita as she went on hunting for her book. She was getting really fractious now and began to tip everything out of her case on to the floor in a mad panic. "I can't possibly do the project properly if I don't find that text-book," she groaned. "It's crucial."

"I know just how you feel love. I felt just the same when I found my cook-book was missing. That recipe was crucial – I wanted to copy it out for our Marilyn. She'd planned to use it for a get-together ... " Mam gave Rita a long sad look full of meaning. "Do you think it could have got mislaid in your bedroom?"

Rita looked startled: "Er – what, mam? Your cook-book or my project book?"

Mam didn't answer.

Rita began to sense some sort of connection. Then she recovered and said: "Impossible for my project book to be in my bedroom, I never even opened the case there."

"Maybe it's the Port Street ghost at it again ... " said Humph.

Jonny came in: "Ghost?" he asked. For some reason he just couldn't resist that word – even though not many people *really* believed in ghosts.

"It seems to have stolen one of our Rita's school books," remarked Humph. "Just like we once thought it had made off with the rabbit book."

Rita spun round at him: "Don't say *you've* hidden it!" she gasped.

"Not in my line, Rita. But you do rather invite stupid tricks at times ... " Humph's monkey face wrinkled cheekily.

Jonny didn't like family rows dragging on and he felt a bit sorry for Rita now. She was clearly quite upset about the loss of her beloved text-book.

"I'll go and see if I can find it ... " he muttered – little realising what danger these few small compassionate words might cause.

Rita looked as if the truth of the universe had dawned when Jonny innocently uttered those kind words as, flaring with suspicion, she began to follow him softly upstairs.

He was so busy concentrating on doing his good deed of retrieving her book from its deep resting place that he never even suspected he was being watched as he squirmed and burrowed to reach it.

At last his fingers curled round its corners, and heaving the mattress up slightly against his shoulders he began to hump himself back into the daylight again. He was quite breathless. He was glad he'd got it back before she found out!

All of a sudden he became aware of slight breathing just at the back of him. Someone was standing there. He froze.

Then, bolstering his courage, he spun round quickly and was met immediately by the blazing face of Rita!

# 6
# The Victor

It was the afternoon at school next day and – wonder of wonders – Jonny was sitting in the classroom happily reading his rabbit library book. Pam was next to him with a book about kites and a large piece of thin white paper with her own drawing of a kite on it.

After his encounter with Rita yesterday it was a sudden change of fortune. Mam herself had followed Rita upstairs with some more stealthy footsteps, and just as Rita was about to grab Jonny and give him a good thumping mam had grabbed Rita by the scruff of her collar and told her to go back to Mavis's IMMEDIATELY and return the lost property. Even dad helped by opening the front door very wide for Rita to get moving and she roared out of the house like a thundering tornado.

The classroom was blissfully quiet. It was the end of a very full day. They had all been to the baths, made terrific resounding crashing noises – enough to make the school fall down – in the music session, and hung upside down in the hall in PE. So now, most of them felt over-restful. And although some work books were open, people like the Browns were sucking sweets and playing with paper darts.

"You should be reading your library books like everyone else if you've finished your Nature Diaries," remarked Miss Broom. Then she said, fluttering her eyelids slightly, "I expect you all to stay quiet and well-behaved whilst I'm away having a word with Mr Hobbs about some new Venetian blinds. He is also going to give me the full details of our Kite Competition – "

There was a strong rustle of excitement.

"We shall all be able to plan, make and test our home-made kites during the coming holidays." Miss Broom took a deep breath and smiled enthusiastically: "Perhaps our class will make the best kites of all – and even win the competition!"

"What sort of a kite are you going to make, Jonny?" breathed Pam when Miss Broom had gone.

But for once Jonny didn't show much interest: "If I get Benny Buck to look after, there might not be enough time or even *room* to make kites. I can't see them letting me keep a rabbit and make a kite all at the same time in our house ... " He frowned slightly. The rabbit had been all that mattered a few days ago and now it was changing to kites.

"I'm glad we're having the kite contest," said Pam smiling. "My mum and dad won't mind that."

Jonny was silent, he didn't like to admit – even to Pam – that he *still* hadn't got mam and dad to sign the permission form for Benny. Any sensible person would have rated his chances of looking after the rabbit at about a thousand to one, when you considered the reasons for *not* looking after it as outlined by the rest of the Briggs family.

And at this very moment the twins were making the tension even worse. They were getting bored with planning kites so they decided to torment Jonny instead as they showed off their rhyming prowess:

> "Jonny Briggs is very funny ...
> All he wants is a big white Bunny,"

they chanted.

When Miss Broom came back they were sitting on top of their desks sending paper darts back to the Browns. "Get down at once," cried Miss Broom sharply. "Josie and Jinny, don't you ever do *any* work?"

Jinny looked indignant. She gave a big gasp of astonishment. "You *know* we do, Miss Broom!"

"We've been doing our poems, miss," said Josie. "You said we could always be doing our poems if we'd nothing else to do."

Miss Broom nodded her head suspiciously: "Yes, it's nice to think you're working at your poetry."

"They just do silly rhymes, Miss Broom," Lily Spencer called out.

Then a voice shouted: "My brother made a slide – slipped on his bumble-bees and nearly died. Bumble-bees is rhyming slang for knees, miss."

"At least you can tell the difference between different styles," said Miss Broom. "Now, let's get back to the kites, shall we?"

Jonny breathed a sigh of relief then to his dismay heard Josie chirping up again: "Please miss, we've got a *proper* poem, can we just read it if we're quick?"

"Hurry up then," sighed Miss Broom, as they both began to giggle.

"Jonny Briggs is mad on rabbits
Rabbits do not like *his* habits
Rabbits always like us twins
And the twins are going to win ... "

They sat down quickly in a strange silence.

"I'll bet they copied it out of a book, Miss Broom," shouted Brian, one of Jonny's supporters, with helpful inspiration.

"It was a very good attempt," said Miss Broom, "and I can see that it hasn't been copied from a book, but in your next poems I think you should keep away from rabbits and Jonny Briggs or any other member of this class." And to stress this point she asked them all to write about kites for their next poetry lesson.

That afternoon after school Jonny was uneasily aware of the consent form still resting – all crumpled-up now – in his pocket. He must get it signed today, he *must*. Especially after that awful episode with the twins – even though most of the class had been on his side.

When he went into the backyard at home, Razzle was there and dad was kneeling down setting some seeds in the soft, black, silty soil.

"Hello son," said dad cheerfully. "Been working hard?" Jonny smiled and stood there hesitating, as dad made a small line in the soil with a trowel.

"I forgot to give you the form to sign, dad … " Jonny drew out the crumpled piece of paper.

"Form? What form?" Dad's mood changed. If there was one thing he couldn't stick, it was signing forms.

"From school. About the rabbit. About me looking after it in the holidays. We have to get the form signed, saying you agree." Jonny's voice rose pleadingly and eagerly. "I know all about how to look after it. An' if you could help us to make the hutch … " His heart fell as he saw dad beginning to scowl heavily.

"I don't know son … " groaned dad. "I just don't know, and that's the truth. Maybe you'd better ask your mam … "

Jonny's hopes sank to rock bottom. Without another word he pocketed the form and walked gloomily into the house. Mam wasn't there.

He went outside again into the sunshine. "Mam's

not there, dad. I've got a pen. Couldn't you sign it dad? It'd only take a tick ... *please*, dad. It's an honour to look after Benny Buck."

"An honour that we might not want, son," said dad wisely. Then he said: "Don't you think you've got enough with Razzle? Where on earth could you keep it really safe round here? It'd have to have a bit of a run round, and dogs and rabbits don't exactly see eye to eye ... "

It was one of those fateful tea-times when everyone was there, even Sandra, as Jonny prepared to give mam the consent form. He knew it was now or never – because mam spent so much time bobbing about before and after tea. But now she was actually sitting down herself and eating a thin slice of bread and butter while Sandra poured her out a cup of tea.

"Perfect peace at last," she sighed as she smiled rather weakly at them all. And then her face tightened up and the smile vanished completely. A strange bit of crumpled paper was being edged towards her from Jonny's side of the table, like a frail and battered boat sailing between the cups and plates.

"It's the rabbit consent form, our mam," Jonny tried to make his voice seem bright and ordinary.

Mam was surprisingly quiet: "It's no good, son. I'm just *not* signing it." But it didn't take long for the general hullabaloo to start up, once Rita began to air her views.

"Good for you, mam! That school should be

ashamed of itself allowing innocent rabbits to be sent to their doom! If a rabbit so much as enters our backyard, *I* as a responsible member of society shall let it escape immediately!"

"And be immediately run over in Port Street," groaned Humph realistically. "I can't see the responsibility of turning out a poor, frightened, dazed rabbit into an alien world of pavements, Princey's dog, and a hundred vans, lorries and cars as such a wonderful human act, our Rita. So you better *hadn't do* it? Right?"

They both glared at each other.

"It's a lot of fuss an' bother about nowt if you ask me," chirped Albert, hastily swallowing a large unchewed lump of rather scratchy crust like a conveyer belt tipping rocks into a dark hole. "I could think of lots of things to do with rabbits without letting 'em escape. What about all the ones they want for conjurers to take out of top hats? We could make a mint. You want to get that school one as quick as lightning, our Jonny – and we'll put it in with that rabbit of Princey's across the road for a bit. Then once it has some babies of its own we can start a Conjurer's Rabbit Market."

"It's name's *Benny Buck*, Albert," Jonny looked round cautiously. "Miss Broom said buck rabbits are the *fathers* not the mothers."

Mam began to finish her tea hurriedly: "Really Albert I just don't know how you manage to think up such a load of drivel! It's a pity you don't use your brain for more suitable occupations!'' Then she put her coat on and said she was going across to Hemlington to visit Marilyn. ''That puppy's far from well after its accident and Marilyn's taking it quite badly.''

The paper from school was still resting like a piece of litter on the tablecloth as everyone moved from the tea-table. Jonny picked it up and put it back in his pocket again. He was thoroughly fed up as he went outside to talk to Razzle in the yard. But he didn't talk to Razzle about the rabbit. He somehow thought it wasn't the right subject to talk to a dog about. Also, there was another point to think about: supposing Razzle was *jealous*? Dogs and even cats could get quite jealous of new arrivals.

He stood dolefully in the backyard for a few seconds. It was a nice evening. Nice and light with a breezy, pale blue sky. And somewhere in the direction of Albert Park he could see a small bird-like object hovering haphazardly in the air. A kite! Perhaps it was someone from their class? He hurried off to the park to find out, with Razzle.

By the time he'd gone through the park gates his spirits were back to normal. He always went in at the boating-pool end where great sounds of quacking ducks and chirping birds always greeted him. It was a cheerful, lively world. Razzle sniffed the path and wagged his tail.

Jonny began to run along the smooth tarmac paths towards the open grass, and in the distance he saw

Peter and Pam and Lily Spencer all holding kites.

Peter's was an old red-and-yellow cotton one that his dad had given him. Lily Spencer's was a plastic one advertising the Red Cross, and Pam's was a bird kite. None of them was home-made.

"We're trying to find out what makes them fly," said Pam. "For when we start to make our own." Then she said: "I had an idea at tea-time. Jonny. Why don't you make a *Rabbit* kite, with ears like wings? I asked dad, and he said we could use our garden shed, if you haven't enough space at home."

Jonny's eyes began to sparkle: a rabbit kite! Nobody in the whole world would have one of those! "I could *try* ... " he said cautiously.

Then he told her about the sad fate of the consent form. "I don't think it's going to work out after all ... "

On the way back home from the park, Jonny said to Razzle: "A rabbit kite ... how about that then? A flying rabbit. No one could grumble at that ... " Razzle cocked his ears – he looked really pleased.

But when they reached home all the joy suddenly faded, for as Jonny walked into the living-room he knew that something was seriously wrong. Mam was back from Marilyn's. She was looking very worried, sitting there silently, all on her own. "Little Chummy is dead." The words came out very sharp and abrupt.

Jonny's spirits sank. Fancy such a nice little puppy dying! He could hardly believe it. He suddenly felt extra thankful that he still had Razzle.

"It's a real shame, mam," he said quietly.

"The trouble is," said mam in a sad, thoughtful voice as if she was talking to Jonny's grandma or someone more her own age, "it's not going to do Marilyn any good. She's very highly strung underneath all that cheerfulness, and it's hard for her – not being out at work. It's lonely stuck in that nice house all day on a new housing estate, and Chummy's been a real companion. I don't want her getting all depressed now he's gone ... "

Jonny nodded. He knew *he* wouldn't like to live away from the town and the park and all his friends.

"What she *really* needs," said mam, "is another little dog straight away to keep her mind off it all for a bit ... "

Jonny nodded again. It sounded a good plan ...

"So I've got this idea ... " said mam slowly. "I've just been thinking, love – how would it be if we let Razzle go to Marilyn's house for a holiday? Marilyn could collect him in her Mini? Just – say – for the school holidays? After all, love you're usually playing out all the time and – "

With dawning horror, Jonny began to realise just what her words meant: "But that's just when Razzle plays the most, too, mam. It's *his* holiday as well. It's the time he goes to the park the most. Marilyn's house is too posh for him. She'd make him lie in that dog basket all squashed up next to her tumble drier ... and he'd *never* be able to get a game of footy ... "

"What a funny thing to say, son!" gasped mam indignantly. "Razzle would probably like a holiday with Marilyn in her lovely little house. She'd treat him like royalty. She always bought Chummy the most expensive dog food."

"He doesn't want to be treated like royalty," cried Jonny fiercely. "An' he likes proper bones from the butchers. He wants a proper dog's life in Port Street, with all his friends. What about *Razzle's* friends, our mam? What about Long Legs and Woofy?"

Mam sensed she was beginning to lose, and so in desperation she played her ace card. "Maybe if you were extra kind and thoughtful and allowed Razzle to stay with Marilyn for a while, son, I could sign that form about your school rabbit. Then you could look after it while Razzle's away ..." Mam smiled encouragingly.

Jonny looked thoroughly miserable. Who would have dreamed it would all have worked out like this? Having to make a choice between his beloved Razzle and Benny Buck.

"I'd sooner keep Razzle here, in his proper place," he pleaded – for somehow he felt mam had already caught him in a sort of web. "And even if you do sign the consent form, mam – it doesn't mean I'll definitely get him. Nearly all the class wants to look after him, and the twins are absolutely *determined* to get him ... "

"I'm determined, too." Mam reached for the pen in her bag. "Give us that form. Let's get it done with."

Slowly and reluctantly, Jonny fetched the ball of

screwed-up paper from his pocket and smoothed it out for mam to sign.

Then, to hide his tears, he went straight out to the yard and stared mournfully at Razzle. He didn't care, one fig – or button – if he never saw that school rabbit again. And yet . . . and yet . . . he knew for a fact that he'd definitely hand in the form. Yes, he'd certainly do that much.

# 7
# Lucky Dip

Miss Broom was sitting at her desk looking through the signed Rabbit Permission slips in front of her. "There are sixteen people who want to look after Benny in the holidays," she announced. "It is pleasing to see how much you all care for pets." Then she added: "But it is not pleasing to see certain people pulling faces at each other."

"Please miss," said Josie, "you'd better let me and Jinny take it, then you'll be really sure it isn't going to be starved. The Browns'll give it newspaper to eat, Miss Broom. They fed their kitten on newspaper and it was sick all over the place."

Jonny and Pam and half the class sprang to the defence. "Please Miss Broom – they made a paper ball for their kitten to *play* with and it chewed some off and was sick." In seconds the Brown brothers had produced loads of curled-up orange peel from their desks ready for a hurling match.

"We'll feed the rabbit properly," said Jinny, "because *we* can get free straw from Sid's Greengrocers *and* old cabbage and cauliflower leaves."

"Please Miss Broom," shouted Jonny desperately, "it wouldn't get *old* cabbage leaves at our house. It would be proper cabbage that our dad grows, and raw carrots and fresh dandelion leaves, and our dad's helping me make a proper hutch for it." Jonny was back in the fray, as he hoped against hope that he would be the one to be chosen.

"It's lies again, miss," howled the twins. "Our hutch won't be in a backyard in a place with rain dripping through the roof giving it rheumatics ... "

"Right ... " said Miss Broom, putting up her hand in the STOP sign. "You seem to have aired that lot quite sufficiently, so now I think we'll start to sort out how we really *are* going to choose Benny's holiday guardian." Miss Broom nodded towards Nadine and asked her to bring the blue plastic bucket from under the Nature table.

Then she said to Nadine and Peter: "You two can help fold up all these consent forms and we'll put them in the bucket and have a lucky dip." She looked round the class. "Hands up those who *aren't* wanting to take the rabbit home?" She smiled at Pam: "Pam. You can be the dipper."

There was an outraged howl from the twins: "PAMELA DEAN! You can't have her, Miss Broom! She'll fish out Jonny Briggs's paper."

"She won't be able to see the papers." Miss Broom looked at them calmly, "She will be blindfolded."

"I've got a blindfold, miss," called Martin Canebender eagerly. He rooted about in his pocket and produced a large grey woolly sock with shoe laces tied to each end. "It's what I use for three-legged races – but you can borrow it."

Miss Broom took a clean, neat, spotted green silk scarf from her drawer and tied it round Pam's head so that she couldn't see.

"Make sure you turn her round *ten* times," called the twins suspiciously, as Miss Broom turned Pam round three times. And even that was a bit too much because Pam became so dizzy she put out her arms and tried to grab Miss Broom's head instead of the sides of the bucket.

"It's still not fair, miss," persisted Josie, amidst groans from everyone else. "She'll be able to feel the wrong bit of paper. Jonny Briggs's paper was crumpled-up paper ... all different from the rest ..."

Miss Broom gave a big sigh. "Never let it be said it's not completely fair," she said. Then she ordered Martin Canebender to bring the orange plastic gloves they used for cleaning out the rabbit hutch so that Pam could put them on. "As you can all see," she pointed out, "Pam will have great difficulty in feeling much with *those* on ..."

Awkwardly, Pam dipped into the bucket and managed to grab a bit of paper which immediately fell to the floor.

Miss Broom picked it up quickly and smoothed it out. It was a faint grey shade and the paper had a lined and ancient feel to it.

"The owner of this consent form is Jonny Briggs," she announced. Then – quickly, before the howls of rage and pain and "We Was Robbed" began to flow – she said: "And don't any of you say it wasn't fair! It is what is known as a coincidence." Miss Broom then wrote the word COINCIDENCE on the board. "It is a word you can all copy into your word dictionaries. It is when something unbelievable happens ... by chance."

Popularity is a strange phenomenon, for suddenly Jonny Briggs was popular with everyone. The Lucky Dip had awarded him its star prize, so everyone crowded round him smiling and friendly in the hope that a bit of his luck would rub off on them.

"Will you be able to get Benny home all right?" asked Miss Broom.

She produced one of those special carriers you can get at the vet's for carrying pets. It was like a flat piece of cardboard at first, but if you followed the instructions and folded it in the right places it made a cardboard carrier complete with handles.

"Can I help him carry the hutch, please, Miss Broom?" asked Suni Nanda. His dark eyes were shyly hopeful. He was new to Jonny's class and his

78

dad ran a skirt and jeans stall on the market at Stockton – but Miss Broom knew that his grandad had once played cricket in India.

Jonny nodded thankfully. He was glad it was Suni. He was a very careful person and had long arms and always won the running and jumping games. He lived just round the corner near Mamoud's shop.

Miss Broom said it was best to take the school hutch in case the other one at home wasn't quite ready.

"And don't forget," she warned, "this is a trial period. If you feel it isn't working out, let me know and I'll give it to someone on our reserves list. Probably Yumna because she knows such a lot about caring for pets."

Yumna smiled happily. She had black frizzy hair and huge dimples and was a good swimmer. The twins pulled the most horrible faces they could think of but she took no notice. She had three brothers who could pull even worse faces.

"He must weigh a ton!" gasped Jonny to Pam when Benny was safely in his cardboard carrier.

"I'll help you with him," said Pam. "The three of us can take it in turns with the hutch and the carrier. We'll keep stopping for rests." Then she said: "I hope Benny and Razzle make friends really quickly."

Jonny's face clouded. He hadn't told anyone about his bargain with mam – about letting Razzle stay at Marilyn's, but on the way home carrying the heavy box with Pam, and with Suni beside him carrying the hutch he began to cheer up again.

"Thanks for helping," he said excitedly as they reached home.

"Phew ... what a journey!" said Pam, as they looked round for the best place to put the rabbit hutch in Jonny's backyard.

"What about that small wooden table in the corner by the wall?" suggested Suni.

Jonny nodded. Never again would mam be able to say that her old wooden table was "neither use nor ornament".

They put the hutch on the table. It fitted just right. Then they opened the hutch, and the three of them hauled the carrier close to it. Opening the top, they swiftly heaved Benny into the hutch in a scuffle of warm furry plumpness and closed the hutch door quickly. And as Pam and Suni dashed back to their own homes, Jonny felt a sudden sense of peace and relief descend.

Mam was actually taking a photograph! It was an event as rare as a trip to the moon. Benny Buck was happily munching away at some carrot in his small private garden outside "Rabbit Villa". "I never realised what sweet little things they are," she said to the rest of the family. They all stared down at the whiskered velvety munching jaws and long delicate ears with mild curiosity.

"The rabbit's a lot bigger than I imagined," said dad bluntly. "My grandad used to breed rabbits for food to sell at the market when he was a lad. His mother used to make him get out early and earn a few coppers with them to keep the family funds up." Then he looked a bit embarrassed as all eyes focused on him.

"Well I never, love," said mam. "I've never heard you tell that story before ... Your grandmother always did strike me as being a very hard woman."

"The reason this rabbit's so big, dad," said Albert, "is because it's grossly over-fed. If I was given half of what he gets, I'd have the strength to become a millionaire. An' that wire netting's not high enough either. It's a good job Razzle's not here, he'd have soon made short rabbit work of it. Talk about serve-yourself meals for enterprising dogs ... "

Jonny sighed and bowed his head. "I wish Razzle *was* here," he muttered. "He'd never eat a rabbit in a month of Sundays."

"Don't you be too sure," hooted Albert derisively; "It's part of the laws of nature for animals to eat each other. An' don't forget I want a *giant* beefburger for tea an' not one of those micro-dots."

Then they all turned slowly round and ambled back into the house, leaving Benny in his new holiday home.

For a few minutes, all was silence – except for the noise of distant traffic and a few yells from people playing about in the street. It was all warm and pleasant and normal with a faint waft of shepherd's pie gently scenting the air from someone's oven.

Then gradually a small sound began to grow from the region of the wooden backyard door. It was a strange, whimpering, scraping noise. A persistent scrabbling and pushing, then a gentle growl followed by a sudden excited yelp as the door was finally shoved open.

It was Razzle!

He began to sniff round the yard energetically; wagging his tail twenty to the dozen. Then, sniffing his way to the rabbit compound he stood on his hind legs against the wire netting and gave an anxious, whimpering, half-excited, puzzled yelp. Then for some unknown reason perhaps personal to Razzle himself, he disappeared out of the yard again like a mysterious and secret visitor ...

"The only thing I wish," said Jonny to Pam the next day at school while they were drawing their kite plans, "is, I wish our Razzle hadn't had to go to Marilyn's. It's somehow spoilt everything. I mean ... Benny's very nice and all that and he's happy and I can feed him, but somehow he's not the same as Razzle ... "

Pam nodded. "They can't do things like play football can they? Except perhaps with their noses and a ping-pong ball." She began to colour her kite drawing bright blue, with the word PAM left all white on it.

"I expect in some ways though it's just as well Razzle's on his own holidays because it means you'll have more time to make a kite for the school competition, Jonny … " She gazed admiringly at his own kite plan. It was an extremely strange shape …

"It looks like that because I'm not putting the ears on it till the very last minute," he whispered. "We don't want *them* copying us … " He glanced quickly at the twins, and was just about to aggravate them by flicking them a note across with "We are the Greatest" scrawled on it, when Mr Badger came into the classroom.

It was extremely rare for the headmaster to be strolling about at this time of the day. He was usually phoning the council offices about the state of the ceilings, talking to Mr Box, the caretaker about some prowlers in the night, or interviewing parents on the mysteries of how *not* to do their children's homework. But today he had on his old suit and comfortable shoes – so they all knew it was a good sign. The only time to worry was when Mr Badger wore his newest striped *grey* suit and his pale-blue shirt and awful black-and-gold striped tie and brown leather shoes.

Mr Badger beamed at them: "I expect you're all wondering why I'm here. I just thought I'd walk round and say a personal word about the School Kite Competition. You can all learn a lot from making kites and it will give you something extra interesting to do in the school holidays. There is one very large country where they have special kite festivals. Can anyone say where it is?"

Yoko put her hand up. "Please sir, is it China?" It

was the first time she had ever put her hand up. Her parents ran Tung's restaurant and takeaway in the town centre, and she said she wanted to be a doctor when she grew up.

Mr Badger looked very pleased and nodded. He knew a terrific lot about all the countries of the world yet he never had the time or the money to go to any of them.

Then – as an extra – to be sure he'd get a good response to his kite contest, he said: "In some places in the world they even used to have kite battles. They used to put reeds in their kites that made strange noises and … "

He was just going to launch into some rather interesting but bloodthirsty accounts of kite battles, when he stopped. He could see that all eyes were fixed on him with glowing, magnetic interest …

"Ahem … Well I think that's all for now, Miss Broom. I always find this class to be particularly responsive to new ideas."

He slipped hurriedly out into the corridor – hoping he hadn't stirred them up *too* much. He wouldn't have put it past them for someone to invent a flying rock disguised as a kite.

The minute he'd gone the whole class was alive with a new enthusiasm and the word *"battle"* trembled excitedly on everyone's lips.

"He doesn't mean real battles," explained Miss Broom hastily. "We don't want any accidents or destruction of property – it would spoil everything."

But an underground thread of preparations was already beginning to take place.

"Our lot against Class Five," whispered the Brown brothers. "Our lot in the park against them: A KITE BATTLE in the holidays!"

"The only thing about *that* is," said Pam doubtfully to Jonny, "we might spend ages making beautiful kites. Then they could all be battered to bits in a kite battle ... "

"We could always make *two* kites," said Jonny, who was now as enthusiastic as the Browns. "We could have our special school ones and a battle one as well ... "

Pam looked unpersuaded. "It *might* be good. But it might be awful ... "

But Jonny had no doubts that it would be terrific. And as he hurried home from school after leaving Pam, he already had a picture of Class Five running for their lives across the grass in Albert Park in ignominious defeat ... He was so wrapped up in all this that when he got to his backyard he wasn't giving any other thing a single thought.

Then he stopped, and came back to the real world. For straight in front of him, as large as life itself, was Razzle – wagging his tail!

# 8
# Flying High

"What a clever, faithful dog! You deserve the Golden Bone Award for escaping from lonely kitchens and tumble driers," Jonny patted and stroked him. What wonderful luck to have Razzle back in his proper home so soon!

They both went dashing into the house together – straight to the biscuit tin, then Jonny popped Razzle back into the yard again, gave him a dish of water and went upstairs to read a comic in complete bliss.

He never even gave his *other pet* a thought! Never even glanced in its direction. As far as he was concerned, everything was all in place – just as he'd wanted it at the beginning of the rabbit rumpus.

The house was dead quiet. No sign of mam or

Marilyn so, yes ... by some method Razzle *had* got back on his own ...

Humph was the next person to arrive, as Jonny told him the news. "He's a real Kool Kustomer," said Humph, laughing. "You'll never have to worry about him looking after himself, our Jonny."

But when mam came in, the atmosphere changed. "It just can't have come all that way on its own! Are you sure it isn't another stray black-and-white dog? He's very common-looking. There's hundreds like him wandering the streets. Are you certain Marilyn isn't somewhere about with her Mini?"

"Razzle isn't at all like other black-and-white ones! He's very knowing, mam. He can find his way better than we can. How would *you* have liked to have lived in that dog-basket next to our Marilyn's tumble drier and only had a toy bone to chew?"

"Bones to chew?" called Albert as he came in through the backyard. "Don't say I'm going to be driven to that." Then he added jubilantly as he caught up with the gist of the news: "So the fat will be on the fire now won't it? What chance of *happy-bunny* life now?"

BENNY BUCK! Jonny felt as if someone had dropped a banger behind him as he charged into the yard to check up. His heart was thumping as a small round gap in the wire netting caught his gaze ... as if some creature had burrowed out ... or in? He stared at the open hutch. It was empty. Then he turned and looked at Razzle. Razzle was completely ignoring him as he slowly and carefully *licked his jaws*. Jonny felt slightly dizzy. It couldn't be right? It just couldn't. Not *Razzle*?

"You look quite green, love," said mam as he shuffled miserably back into the house.

He looked down at the ground in silent, gnawing pain. It just *wasn't* true. It couldn't be. His mouth felt dry. He couldn't even bear to tell anyone of his fears.

"I think I'd better go across and ask Dora if I can use their phone to speak to our Marilyn," muttered mam anxiously. (Dora was Mrs Prince and she let them and some other neighbours use her phone for emergencies.)

"It looks as if your mam's gone for good," said dad, as he ate his tea in tense silence and stared irritably at Mavis and Rita who were getting every ounce of drama out of the dreadful tale of Razzle's free meal.

"He didn't even leave a scrap of fur anywhere, Mavis. He must have swallowed the poor creature whole! He'll hardly be able to walk ... "

"Didn't he even leave any paws to make Lucky Rabbit Paw brooches?" asked Mavis timidly. "Granny had this lucky rabbit's paw brooch all decorated with beads by the Red Indians ... "

"Isn't it time you two were getting out to the muscle-hunting?" asked dad brusquely. "It seems to be growing a bit squashy in here with all these bodies milling around. It doesn't give much space for the reading of newspapers ... I think it's me that needs a lucky foot in this house ... to kick some folk out." He stopped as he heard mam's voice. She was back again.

Jonny could hear his mother standing at the front door, talking. She was saying: "Thank you very much, Harold. You've taken a big weight off all our minds. Will you want the cardboard box back?"

He was puzzled. How could Harry Prince possibly be taking a big weight off *their* minds?

"It's that wretched rabbit!" said mam as she walked into the living-room bearing a box. Her voice was a mixture of relief and exasperation. "Their Harold nipped round our back earlier on today and found Razzle there looking at Benny as if he'd just come upon a free dinner at the Ritz. So he rescued it until we were all back home and put it in a box next to his own rabbits. Now that's what I call a kind and thoughtful act ... "

Then she added: "Oh yes, Albert. And he said that if we wanted to reward him you could give him two green George the Fifth stamps as a swap for a Christmas 1984 stamp."

"You don't say!" chuntered Albert grumpily. "Might have known there was a Princey catch in it somewhere. He's got a cheek! He should have left it where it was and let fate look after it."

"Well," said Humph cheerfully, "you've got both the rabbit *and* Razzle now, Jonny. It's all back to square one. Happy?"

Jonny nodded and smiled, then he hesitated. "I

am sort of . . . " He looked at them all and gave a slight gulp. "The trouble is, I like Benny, and all . . . an' I'm glad I've got it to look after . . . But . . . " He gave a sigh . . . it had all been so complicated. Who would have thought that looking after one small rabbit would have caused so much fuss?

"But what, son?" asked mam.

"Mam!" exclaimed Rita. "You *pander* to him! Can't you see how he's just loving every second of being the centre of attention? He's getting into a proper little spoilt brat. It's all due to him that we've had this mix-up. And it's only by grace and good fortune that Princey saved that poor defenceless little animal!"

"Why not let Princey keep the school rabbit as a reward," suggested Albert smartly. "To put with his own, as a present for saving it from Razzle – instead of giving him some of Albert Briggs's oldest and rarest stamps that he isn't going to get anyway."

"Never mind them chipping in, Jonny," pressed Humph. "Just you say what you really think."

Jonny looked a bit shy and uncomfortable – but he took the plunge: "The thing is – that our class are going to be able to make *kites* during the school holidays, and me and Pam Dean want to make the best ones and she says I can do mine in their shed – if there isn't enough room here . . . But I'd sooner make it in our backyard." He stopped, then added after a heavy silence: "But will there be enough space, with two pets there, to fix up a proper kite?"

"Serves you right then, doesn't it?" purred Rita. "P'raps it'll teach you to be less greedy in future. Mam told you not to have that rabbit in the first place."

"She never," gasped Jonny defensively. "She signed the form so Marilyn could have – "

"That's all water under the bridge now," chipped in mam quickly. There were signs of tempers beginning to rise again.

"Cool down," said Humph calmly. "What about *this* for an idea … "

They all looked at him and began to listen like drowning men grasping at straws.

"It strikes me," explained Humph, wrinkling his monkey brow, "that the ideal place for Benny Buck – would be at *our Marilyn's*. It would be just the right size for her garden, and seeing as how Razzle couldn't stick it and came back home, she could have Benny for company instead. Our Jonny could still look after it and go and visit and see it's OK especially as mam's already there almost every second. So how about it? I'll bet our Marilyn'd be over the moon. She's always liked rabbits."

Mam nodded slowly. "She did once have a Bunny-Rabbit Nightdress Case from her aunty Phyllis when she was little. She liked that *very* much. It wore a little white lacy apron with carrots in its pocket."

"Mother you're THE END," gasped Rita as she grabbed Mavis sharply by the arm. "We can't stand listening to this rubbish any longer!" And they vanished.

"I always knew that Bunny-Rabbit Nightdress Case would do us all a favour some time," said dad, trying to keep his face straight.

"I'll go back to Dora's right now and phone Marilyn to get it sorted out," said mam. "I didn't ring before because of Harold telling me what had happened and bringing the rabbit back. So, second time lucky perhaps?"

She disappeared again, but this time she was back after only a few minutes. "Marilyn's absolutely delighted!" Mam proclaimed. "She said she'd been feeling really miserable because Razzle had vanished and she hadn't the heart to tell us. She just kept hoping he'd turn up again. I think Benny Buck will be just the ticket for Marilyn. It's surprising what a small living creature can do to help lonely people."

Jonny was radiant. His face was covered in one large happy smile when he heard the news. At first he'd felt a bit uncertain about Humph's suggestion. After all, it was the school rabbit, and he knew that you were supposed to let Miss Broom know if you couldn't manage to look after it, so that someone else could have a turn. But this was special. For a start, he'd still be looking after it in an even better place than their yard. For although Marilyn's kitchen was a bit bleak for lively dogs, he knew that her fresh, flowery, grass-filled garden was ideal for rabbits. Added to which, Benny would be giving an extra person a lot of much-needed pleasure, for a week or two, and he, Jonny, could do his kite in the backyard after all.

Then – knowing that he wouldn't be staring very much at Benny Buck from now on – he took his drawing book and a pen and went in the yard and tried to draw him. Tried to see what size his ears *really* were. And whereabouts his eyes were and how big his nose was. So as to have a really good *Rabbit Kite* ...

"The more thoroughly you plan your kites out at school," stressed Miss Broom the next day as Jonny and Pam sat there with their kite sketches and plans on the desks in front of them, "the more exciting it will be to continue your project in the school holidays. You must all get as much as possible into your information and research notebooks. Library books will also be very helpful, plus your own personal experiences and ideas about kites. Your parents too – they may well have some good hints and advice. Shared knowledge is a wonderful thing. Always remember that all the great wonders of the world would not have been possible if people hadn't shared their knowledge."

Miss Broom was slightly breathless after this long speech, as she walked towards the windows and stood in a faint refreshing draft of fresh breezy air. And as she felt the waft of newly-baked bilberry tarts creeping in from the corner ship, it inspired her to continue her theme.

"Just imagine," she suggested, "if no one had tried to produce gas cookers? What would all the mums and dads have done about cooking meals?"

"Microwaves, miss," called Martin Canebender; which was followed by other helpful replies such as: "We never use our cooker, miss. The door dropped off and got used for a sledge in that snowy weather after Christmas."

And: "Please Miss Broom, my mother never cooks. My sister does it all, and all we ever get is spam fritters from the chip shop, an' anyway I only like mashed bananas. I could live on those when I can find the fork ... "

Then Jinny said, very primly: "Please miss – if you *share* how you're doing things – it's just *copying*. And Jonny Briggs'll copy our kites ... he never thinks of his own ideas."

Pam and Jonny could hardly believe their ears!

"What about the Giant Cave?" they howled.

"And making my gold belt!" declared Jonny. "*And* teaching our Razzle to do tricks. And – "

"That is ENOUGH!" warned Miss Broom with an angry spark in her eyes. "I am now coming round to look at your work."

Immediately there was a cooling off period and everyone began to peer at their work as if they had just come across it by accident.

The twins even looked slightly guilty as they started to fold some bits of paper into the shape of kites and colour them. For the truth was they had hardly one idea between the two of them, whereas Jonny and Pam were well away with their plans and drawings.

Miss Broom paused by Jonny's side. "Very good," she looked pleased. "A very good idea, Jonny Briggs."

The twins exchanged long and crafty looks . . .

"If you ask me," whispered Pam to Jonny when Miss Broom had moved on towards Nadine, who was designing a kite with coloured paper streamers flowing from it, "if you ask *me* . . . those twins are up to something. And it's *not* an idea about making kites." Then she frowned and added: "But it could be one about pinching someone else's special ideas . . . "

On the way home, Jonny said: "I just can't wait for the holidays to really try out our kites. Just imagine flying our very own in the park. And – " he gave her a sudden quick look – "*the battle* and all. The kite battle. Don't forget we must make two kites each. Our proper best ones and our battle ones." His eyes glowed with joy, and as he reached his back door he felt a wave of contentment as he carried his orange cardboard folder with his kite plans inside it.

Albert was just raiding the bread-bin when Jonny reached the kitchen. Albert was also complaining about Princey wanting his best stamps. "Those George the Fifths could be the rarest in the whole world one of these days." Albert hesitated as he took a huge bite from a bread bun, then, spotting Jonny's fatal mistake (which had been to put his orange folder on the kitchen table for half a second whilst he stroked Razzle), Albert grabbed the folder and began to look at the plans.

"Who's done all that for you?" he asked cynically.

"No one. We've done it ourselves. It's so as we can make 'em at home in the holidays." Jonny's heart was sinking fast. Albert still had hold of his folder, but he knew it would be fatal to try and grab it back as Albert would just torment him and clear off with it. At times Albert was like a large bouncing dog that grabs a paper or a hat and dashes away with it. Jonny was beginning to learn that the only answer was patience and pretending it didn't matter.

"Good job I've looked at them the first," Albert had now gone all official and knowledgeable – like Mr Corkerdale in the Savings Bank. "Me and Tommy Fitzpatrick are experts. If you lend us them plans I'll take them with me to Tommy's tonight and he'll make you a proper scale model from them." And to Jonny's horror he walked out of the kitchen with the folder still in his iron grip.

So it hadn't paid to be patient after all, thought Jonny as he rushed after Albert with real tears on his cheeks. How could he ever re-do all that work on his kite plans if Albert lost them all at Tommy's house?

"Don't take 'em to Tommy's – *please* don't take 'em there, our Albert," he pleaded.

Albert grinned slowly: "Stop getting so edgy, our kid, Tommy's a genius."

"Then why doesn't he make his own plans?"

yelled Jonny. But Albert just shot out of the house taking Jonny's orange folder with him.

For a few minutes, Jonny felt his whole body shuddering with deep sobs as he trudged upstairs to his bunk. What ever would happen now?

The hours he'd spent planning his rabbit kite … ! The drawings he'd made! The information he'd written down! The lists he'd made about exactly what he'd need and where to get it from! All lost now; all blown to the wind in the direction of Tommy Fitzpatrick's.

And then, as he suddenly caught sight of his gold belt lying half-hidden on top of the toy-box, he began to recover. Why should he lie here sobbing and let Albert get away with the most important plans, he – Jonny – had ever worked at? Lying here wouldn't help one tiny bit. Why should Albert always get away with things?

He toppled off his bunk. He would go to Tommy Fitzpatrick's and ask for his property back immediately! And he'd ask Humph to come with him.

He went in the bathroom and washed his tear-smeared face, and felt better. Then he went downstairs again, just in time to see Humph arriving home.

He watched Humph closely as he came into the house. He was carrying something …

No? Surely? He couldn't believe it … But as Humph dumped his school books on the chair Jonny knew for certain he was carrying the orange folder.

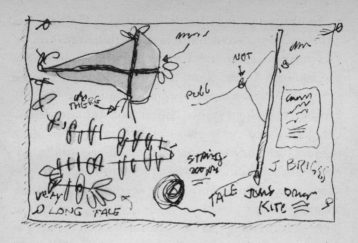

# 9
# Holiday Magic

"I rescued it for you just before the road sweeper slung it in his rubbish bin," smiled Humph. "You must have dropped it on the way home. Never even knew it was yours at first."

Jonny told him about Albert.

"So that was it ... " Humph smiled, then began to laugh. "I saw our Albert outside the paper shop talking to Tommy. They were both eating meat and potato pies and talking about a kite battle, of all things. Tommy's kid sister Evangelina is in Class Five at your school and they're having a sort of battle with this other class in the school holidays and Albert and Tommy have said they'll coach her lot and act as their managers ... What a laugh! It'll end in complete chaos if our Albert's involved." He grinned.

Jonny's eyes went quite large with astonishment. Of course – Evangelina Fitzpatrick: the Brain Box of the Juniors! And to think he'd never even connected her with Albert's mate Tommy Fitzpatrick, her big brother. But there again, Albert had so many different pals. They came and went like a procession of passing traffic. Great, big, stamp addicts; long, thin, aeroplane buffs; large, square, gambling experts; short, bony, computer fanatics; small, plump, fishing wizards; the stream was endless, and gave Albert plenty of other roofs to shelter under when things got a bit cramped or awkward at home, which was mostly all the time. All this, *and* The Tigers.

"I'm glad you got the plans back for me, Humph," said Jonny gratefully. "Just imagine Tommy and Albert using them, and all linked with that kite battle, against *our* class! Class Five is Mr Hobbs's lot and they're always winning things. Just imagine *my* plans being passed on to them by our Albert!"

"Your bunch?" Humph looked stunned. "All you harmless little sprats in Miss Broom's – against old Hobbsey's hooligans? In a *battle*? What's the world coming to?"

"Don't let Albert know it's us, Humph."

"I shan't say a word," replied Humph jokingly. "The whole situation seems too horrible even to contemplate. But I advise you to do one thing ... "

"What?" Jonny looked puzzled. Humph seemed quite serious now.

"Keep a copy of your plans," said Humph.

"A copy?" Jonny wasn't even quite sure what Humph meant. "You don't mean – " His face began to look a bit droopy as he now began to get the meaning: "A copy … not for me to copy it all out again? It would take days and days and I'd be sure to make lots of mistakes! Every time I try to do my best I just seem to make mistakes."

"Everyone does that," replied Humph. "You just have to keep trying. There's a lad in our class that can't speak English properly yet. But he gets top marks for written work and there isn't a single mistake. He spends hours and hours getting it right. He's a miracle!" Then Humph said: "But I know you aren't quite a miracle yet, our Jonny, so what you could do is let me take your folder and I'll get your notes and plans photo-copied for you at our school. Then if anything goes missing again, you won't be sunk. All right?"

"Great!" Jonny nodded happily. "A photo-copy! The only people who ever have those – are teachers and Mr Badger; for when they've thought out Nature Quizzes."

Humph was as good as his promise, and the following day he presented Jonny with a perfect copy of all Jonny's kite plans with never a word said, to keep in case of emergency.

Jonny put them in the drawer underneath his socks and T-shirts. It was a spot where no one else ever went. His things were too small for anyone else.

Later in the week, Jonny told Pam what had happened. It was when they were doing maths.

"It's a photo-copy and it's under my socks and T-shirts. Just imagine, if our Humph hadn't spotted the folder lying in the street! And fancy our Albert and Tommy Fitzpatrick coaching Hobbsey's lot for the kite battle. And imagine his sister being Evangelina Brain Box! I'll bet she'll have a terrific kite... " He felt a tinge of envy.

"Our class don't *need* coaches or managers," said Pam staunchly. "We'll win a kite battle *easily*. And thanks for offering to get my plans copied too, Jonny – but I don't need it. Mine will never disappear. It's just not like that in our house. And they're as safe as sausages in this desk. They're right underneath my school atlas." Her voice faded, as she realised that Miss Broom was already telling them to put away the maths equipment and get out their kite plans.

Jonny and Pam opened their desks eagerly and proudly. They knew Miss Broom would be delighted with their progress. It was good to be doing so well for a change.

But Pam's face suddenly clouded with an awful suspicion ... Her desk wasn't the same as it had been before play-time this morning. The atlas was lying on top of all her other books. And there wasn't a sign of her plans!

Jonny saw her gasp. He looked hastily into his own jumble of a desk. But no orange folder greeted his searching eyes. He began to scrabble about amongst dried-up apple cores and sweet papers and crumpled exercise books. But soon it was obvious that his precious folder had vanished, too.

"Did you put your *name* on your plans, Jonny?" asked Pam, with even more suspicion.

He shook his head: "There was a 'JB' crayoned on the folder though."

" 'JB' could mean anyone," said Pam sadly. "And I did just the same as you, no name on the plans but 'PD' on my folder. They might have vanished for ever."

"So you're saying that they've vanished from *inside* your desks?" said Miss Broom, frowning deeply as they told her the awful news.

They both nodded miserably.

"Pages and pages of work," groaned Jonny. "Drawings, and plans, and writing and calculations."

Miss Broom was extremely annoyed. She knew they'd worked extra well. "Has anyone seen the folders belonging to Jonny Briggs and Pamela Dean?" she asked.

There was a stony silence in the classroom.

"They can't just have vanished into thin air," persisted Miss Broom irritably. Then she said: "Well – I'm very sorry Pam and Jonny. Check up again at home, and anywhere else where they might have been left by mistake. Nevertheless it all seems extremely strange … " She gave every single person in the class a personal and piercing look. "But we cannot waste time having a post-mortem at present or we'll never get our proper work done. I will come round to each of you individually and see how you've been getting on."

Jonny watched her as she moved round the class complimenting people on their progress. He should have been one of those, and Pam. But now they were just outsiders. It wasn't fair!

Miss Broom was standing next to the twins, now. They both had piles and *piles* of work on their desk tops. Double the amount of anyone else!

"All I can say is – I'm pleasantly amazed," smiled Miss Broom. "You must have both worked like little Trojans. The actual drawings and ideas in your kite project are excellent. You should be able to make some really good models in the school holidays." Miss Broom riffled the pages of the work on their desks casually as she still had more work to see. "Some of the writing seems a bit haphazard on *some* of the pages," she remarked. "But I do realise that writing can change dramatically according to what you write with and where you are writing."

The twins were almost bursing with delight. Swank was oozing out of every pore as they bobbed about to make sure they had the full attention of everybody else.

But they didn't look at Jonny Briggs and Pam ...

Then Miss Broom said: "I am going to pin Josie and Jinny's kite drawings on the wall to show others just what can be achieved with a bit of thought."

Jonny saw both of them suddenly shrink as if a cold·

wind was blowing, and he nudged Pam. Then – as Miss Broom began to put the drawings on the wall – they both gasped from sheer disbelief! They were their own first sketches! Not their very precious final efforts still being worked on at home, but the ones they had started with and put a lot of work into.

"They've copied them!" said Pam. "They'll have traced them out at play-time in the girls' toilets!"

By now the twins were looking a bit alarmed. They hadn't really expected Miss Broom to put the work on the wall. They'd just hoped to impress her and get a few buckshee ideas from JB and PD and stick the folders back, later.

"Those plans up there are *ours*, Miss Broom," shouted Jonny indignantly. "They've been stolen!"

"Yours?" Jinny began to laugh mockingly. "They never are! A special person helped us with them – but it certainly wasn't you or Pam Dean! Miss Broom told us to get as much information as we could," babbled Jinny in a bit of a guilty panic, "and this special person called James Billingsgate passed on some plans *he* had done at his school with his friend Patti Dukes."

"Or *J*eremy *B*ear and *P*etronella *D*uck?" suggested the Brown brothers, with amazing brightness as further names with the initials JB and PD filled the classroom. The twins just sat there – glaring and speechless.

Then – knowing they'd been found out and with one last attempt at regaining some sympathy – Josie gave one of her crocodile sobs as she blinked her eyes and rubbed them really hard to try and make a few watery tears appear. "We were only trying to help our class to be best, miss. And you do go on a lot about sharing ideas … "

Miss Broom nodded her head: "Yes – I did say ideas should be shared, but everyone should add their own ideas and use their own brains as well." Then she turned to Pam and Jonny and her eyes twinkled slightly as she said: "And it's because your ideas were so good they got put on that wall in disguise and we found out whose they were!"

"*And* I've got a copy at home, to prove it!" announced Jonny triumphantly.

Miss Broom turned to the twins again: "I shall expect both of you to produce kites in the school holidays that are *not* the same as Pam's and Jonny's. And you'd better give them back all their work immediately."

Slowly and reluctantly Jinny and Josie produced Pam and Jonny's folders and put all the plans back into them again.

"And don't think you're great 'cos you're not," hissed Jinny.

That afternoon at the school gates at home time, Jonny said to Josie: "I just want to know one thing. Are you two joining in the kite battle against Mr Hobbs's class in Albert Park in the holidays or not – seeing you want our class to be best?" (He was asking them because he just couldn't deny they were very good at battles if they were on your side.)

"We might, and we might not," answered Josie with her nose in the air. "And we don't have to tell *you*, anyway – clever clogs. We might even join Mr Hobbs's lot against *you* – so there!"

"Or us and Arrominter Merryweather and Martin Canebender and Bobby Grappler might form our own gang and fight you lot *and* Hobbsey's lot with our new *secret* kite plan that's better than anyone else's in the world." And they both ran off giggling. Then they both shouted at the top of their voices from a distance: "And our kite won't look like a daft old *flying rabbit* either."

Jonny and Pam looked at each other silently. But their eyes were sparkling, for they knew that whichever side the twins decided to join – the kite battle in the park was definitely ON.

When Jonny arrived home it was more obvious than ever that the holiday magic was already beginning as he saw Albert peering into a book called *Air Currents and Wind Velocity*. There was a large piece of tissue paper by his side, along with some string and a few thin strips of wood.

"I expect you're thinking this is a kite for that battle," said Albert sarcastically. "Because in case you don't know it, me and Tommy Fitzpatrick are organising Hobbsey's lot against Broomy's – which I suppose is *you*, as you're in Miss Broom's mob?"

Jonny remained completely and tactfully silent. You had to watch every word with Albert.

"Anyway, if that's what you were thinking, you'd be wrong," Albert continued. "Because this happens to be what's known as an *Extravaganza* for The Tigers. We're setting up again properly and we're going to fly kites with Tigers on them as an advertisement in the holidays. Every day, we'll be seen somewhere – flying our kites and playing mouth-organs, comb and paper and drums with a touch of the bagpipes from Sammy MacTavish."

Jonny nodded carefully.

"The point is," said Albert, "that me and Tommy's got it worked out to make that Kite Battle a really magic day. There's sure to be lots of people watching it all so we'll be able to manage Hobbsey's gang and do our Tigers routine at the same time as an advertisement. Our Humph was daft to have left The Tigers and our Rita wants her head examining not doing the singing act with Mavis. Anyway, it doesn't matter any more, because when Hobbsey's side wins the battle against your lot, Tommy's kid sister Evangelina is going to sing *A Song of Triumph* which she's written herself."

Jonny stood there almost glued to the ground with a creeping horror. What had started off as holiday magic and a sort of friendly unofficial kite battle with Class Five in the park was growing into a gigantic and ominous circus act manipulated by Albert and Tommy. He began to pray for heavy rain to wipe the whole idea out, or for The Tigers to be signed up to go and play at some important occasion: like a Hot-pot

Supper in the North Pole where they'd be stranded for at least a month.

"It all sounds ... er ... very interesting, Albert," he muttered.

"Interesting?" hooted Albert. "It'll be a RAVE-UP!" Then, hastily buttering about ten rich tea biscuits, he hurried away with some very greasy tissue paper.

"So it's the start of the holidays at last, love," said mam to Jonny one evening after tea. "At least I shan't have to worry about you all getting up in time – for a bit. You'll be able to go to Marilyn's more often too. She's really happy looking after Benny. Everything's worked out very well when you come to think of it ... "

Jonny smiled: "Yes mam. I'm glad it worked out well with Benny. Thanks for signing the form, mam."

But as he walked slowly upstairs that night his mind was on other things as he wondered if *they* would work out all right. Things like the sound of Albert's mouth-organ harmonising awkwardly with the noise of a pair of crows flying home to roost, and the creak of Albert's own Extravaganza being hastily tacked together.

Jonny gave a low and desperate sigh ...

# 10
# Charge of the Kite Brigade

For once, the school holiday weather was behaving itself. It was quite warm and sunny and dry. But there was one thing niggling Jonny as Kite Fever took over in the Briggs household; there was hardly any breeze.

Breezy weather was essential for kites. Without a few gusty winds and high billowing white clouds and dappled sunshine, kites could be falling flat on their faces and remaining there.

Teesside was a funny place for weather. It was near the sea and was becalmed from time to time in a pall of pale grey nothingness when not even a bird seemed to fly. But mainly it was the other way and bright and breezy.

Jonny hadn't breathed a word about the Kite Battle lately, and strangely enough neither had Albert. But Jonny's proper project with his huge rabbit kite was going from strength to strength, as dad, mam and even Rita put in their oar to carry it forward; while Humph kept talking about aerodynamics.

It was turning out to be an amazing box shape, and Rita had actually donated some very thin cotton stuff she called cheese cloth that had got ripped from a long white dress.

The box shape had four ribbon-like, dangling paws on its four bottom corners, and it had a face with whiskers painted on and two huge plastic ears sticking out rather like the wings of an aeroplane.

"It's certainly the strangest flying object I've ever seen," said dad in quite envious amazement, "and I only hope it'll do you proud, son, and manage to rise more than two feet from the ground."

"I think it's a lovely memory of how you let our Marilyn look after Benny Buck to comfort her, Jonny love," said mam romantically, "and I hope yours is the best one in the school. It certainly should be, with all our help!"

Jonny was thankful that Albert was out of the house most of the time while the kite was being made, but Albert did drop one broad hint to the effect that he and Tommy were designing a small hot-air balloon and not a kite to advertise The Tigers in the park on Battle Day. "In fact ... " he added, going all brisk, like a real manager, "we might get Hobbsey's lot to turn the whole battle into *water* balloons instead."

Jonny said never a word. He almost pretended he hadn't even heard what Albert said, because he was so anxious not to have the progress of his special school project spoilt by a sudden Albert Deluge. And quite truthfully, the battle idea was beginning to fade a bit into the background – especially with the weather being so calm.

Even Razzle seemed to like Jonny's school kite. He wagged his tail and gave two sharp excited yelps and whimpers as Jonny carried it into the yard to show him.

"An' just you mind you don't ever pounce on it or put your paws through it or bite its ears off," warned Jonny solemnly as he put the kite back in the front room behind a chair and took Razzle to the park to play.

The first people he saw were the Brown brothers feeding some ducks with a stale currant tea-cake, and Pam who was talking to them.

"Come back to our garden shed," said Pam as they left the Browns. "I'll show you how my gi-normous butterfly kite's going on. Our Stew let me borrow some special waterproof paint to colour it."

Jonny had never been in Pam's garden shed before. It was painted with brown creosote and was very neat with rows of hammers, chisels, screw-drivers and garden tools in special fastenings on the walls, and there was an electric lawnmower next to the work bench alongside some boxes with little seeds showing through.

"The seeds are going to be put in the greenhouse at the bottom of the garden," said Pam.

Jonny took a deep breath: a *greenhouse*? Even their Marilyn hadn't got one of those! "You lucky thing having a greenhouse," he breathed. "I'll bet our dad'd like one – except it'd soon get broken."

But Pam said she'd gone off them ever since *her* dad made her wash the windows in it, and she liked garden sheds best ...

"Have you heard any more news about the battle?" asked Pam as she lovingly wound up the string to her kite.

Jonny stared at the seed boxes: "There's a bit of Albert trouble going on," he said. "It's not going to be like it was when we started out. Albert and Tommy are going to ruin the whole thing with this Tigers' Extravaganza and water balloons and things. All *they* want is to advertise the Tigers every way they can think of."

Pam smiled comfortingly: "Cheer up, Jonny. Water balloons might be good fun if it's hot calm weather, like it is now. I was once in a water balloon fight with our Stew. We filled our balloons with water at the park tap. You don't need to fasten them; just hold the water in with your fingers at the top of the balloons, then let fly ... We'll take some balloons and we'll take that old kite I once got at Saltburn – then we'll be ready for anything!"

As battle Saturday drew nearer, Jonny began to get really excited. The word had been passed round only to bring very old kites. He and Pam didn't mention water balloons ... They decided to keep them as their own secret emergency. Their secret weapon against Hobbsey's lot ... in case Hobbsey's lot also had a secret weapon ...

"Whatever are you spending all your pocket money on balloons for?" asked Rita nosily. "You only have those at dances and parties. They're no good in sunny weather. The sun rots them."

"It's for a sort of outdoor party in the park, for our class and Mr Hobbs's class," mumbled Jonny, trying to escape.

"Outdoor party? When? How is it Mavis and I don't know about it if it's out of doors and in the park?"

Jonny shrugged his shoulders.

Then Rita said: "Is it anything to do with that Extravaganza our Albert's doing with The Tigers tomorrow afternoon? Because if it is – you want to keep well away. Mavis and I have just met these two marvellous boys who are both going to be monks and belong to the Noise Abatement Society. Mavis and I are striving for a more peaceful world. We've gone off muscle power."

"Did Albert say anything else about what they were doing?" asked Jonny fearfully.

"Don't ask me. All I know is they've got these messages stuck on trees and things advertising it, and

Mavis and I have spent four hours removing them because we believe in the preservation of trees."

By the time Friday night arrived it was obvious to everyone that something special was about to happen in the park the next afternoon. Even mam mentioned that she might take a walk over there to look at the tulip display with dad, just to see what this Extravaganza was, that Albert had been on about. "As long as the police aren't called in, our Albert," said mam warningly. "That's all I worry about."

"*Police*?" howled Albert indignantly. "It's not a football match!"

Jonny was awake before anyone the next morning and looked out of the bedroom window to gauge the weather. The sky was bright blue and there were wisps of cotton-wool cloud whisking breezily across the chimney pots. It was ideal weather for kites – or anything ...

Straight after breakfast he rushed to the park with Razzle to see if anyone else had rushed there as well – for a check-up of the afternoon plans. Sure enough he saw Pam and the Brown brothers, Yoko, Peter, Lily Spencer and even in the distance – the twins – all tussling with a ragged assortment of kites in practice for the afternoon.

"It'll be a doddle!" yelled the Browns confidently, as they tied an old newspaper kite to a seat, and began to shout out instructions about what was going to happen: "One side goes to the gates end of the grass and the other side goes to the café end, and then this manager from The Tigers – this famous Pop group wot's coming to watch us – will blow the whistle and we just charge ... We have to run like the clappers an' try an' get to the other end still holding on to our own kites, and the side with the most kites still left wins." Then the Brown brothers grinned and said: "Which is *us*!"

Jonny smiled cautiously, pretending he didn't know who the mysterious manager from The Tigers was. Then they raced home to get their dinners golloped down as quickly as possible.

"We'll all meet by the oak tree as quick as we can, after," urged Jonny, hoping that he wouldn't have to go and stand in the queue at the chip shop on this day of all days.

"Would you like to take Razzle with you to the park this afternoon, mam?" he asked anxiously when dinner was over. "I've got something very special to do. He'd like a walk with you and dad. He doesn't mind his new lead a bit ... "

"All right then," said mam, with a sudden streak of good nature. "Something tells me I'm going to enjoy looking at those tulips. It'll be just like your dad and me walking out together when we were courting. I used to take next door's wheezing old bulldog for a stroll so as to meet him in secret."

"In secret, love?" said dad, looking startled. "I never knew that? Didn't they think I was good enough for you?"

Quickly, Jonny took his packet of balloons and rushed back to the park again. Albert hadn't been home for *his* dinner, but as Jonny reached the grass he heard strange sounds coming from behind a privet hedge. And, through a very thin patch in it, he saw Albert playing his mouth-organ and eating a Chinese takeaway.

"If only he'd forget and stay there all afternoon," prayed Jonny, as he hurried towards Pam and the rest of his friends. But his hopes were dashed, for suddenly Albert arrived with The Tigers and began to order everybody about. Jonny was quite thankful that Albert was pretending not to know him as Albert announced himself as the manager in charge of things and asked Josie, one of the twins, to call heads or tails when he tossed a twopenny piece, to decide which ends of the grass each side should be choosing.

Josie was so bowled over by a Tiger speaking to *her*, that she and Jinny promptly decided to put their full weight behind their home depot of Miss Broom's brigade. And both of them were so stunned by Albert's baggy white trousers and orange mock-fur waistcoat and earrings with silver stars on them, that they asked him for his autograph on the backs of their hands. To Jonny's relief Albert scrawled *Top Tiger*, instead of his true name, with a smudgy felt-tip pen.

"You know what?" panted Pam, as she and Jonny hurried towards the café end of the grass with the rest of Miss Broom's class to start the battle: "I've

116

just seen Miss Broom and Mr Hobbs, with tennis rackets ... ''

They both stared at each other in dismay.

"I hope they don't come over here by mistake," said Pam nervously. "They were over there, near the tulip beds ... ''

But Jonny didn't look towards the tulip beds. Oh no! His eyes were nearly popping out of his head as he stood and gaped in stunned silence at what was happening at the other end of their battle field.

The most fantastic contraption they'd ever seen was arriving. It was an old wooden truck painted with yellow-and-black tiger stripes, and above it – hovering in the sky – was a small, bright yellow, hot-air balloon with *Tigers* written on it. The balloon was fastened to the truck by a very, very long thread.

"That truck's big enough to carry the whole of the Hobbs brigade on it!" gasped Jonny. "It's even got rails to tie their kites to!" He groaned helplessly: "We haven't got a hope against all that. It's just like a huge charging Man O' War ... ''

"Their Secret Weapon ... '' said Pam – feeling as hopeless as Jonny as their whole group stood there powerlessly. Then, in a sudden flash of inspiration, she said: "What about *our* secret weapons then?"

Everyone looked puzzled, except for Jonny.

"*The balloons!*" he yelled. He pulled the packet from his pocket and tipped them out on the grass. "Grab one and get to the tap," he howled. "Fill all the balloons with water!"

There was a mad scramble as everyone grabbed a balloon and dashed for the tap at the edge of the grass near the Parkie's hut. The only people who didn't dash were the twins.

"You two stay here to guard our kites. Tell Top Tiger we've forgotten something – and not to blow his whistle to start till we're back."

For once the twins nodded like little lambs as they waited to contact Top Tiger with the message, and receive a toothy smile from the glamorous Albert Briggs. And Hobbsey's lot were so busy fiddling with their Man O' War truck and their kites, that they never saw Broomy's titchies assembling their secret water balloons …

And not a single person on *either* side noticed the lady in blue tennis shorts and the man in the grey track suit who were grumbling about the tennis courts being full.

But Miss Broom and Mr Hobbs had certainly noticed *them*. "I can see that little horror Briggs and all his cronies from your class, and they're *up to no good*, Kathleen," said Mr Hobbs.

Miss Broom gripped her tennis racket firmly: "And *I* can see Evangelina Fitzpatrick and all *your* little demons up to no good on that old wooden truck." Then she added softly: "I thought you said Evangelina Fitzpatrick was the most ladylike girl in your class? So how is it she's waving her arms about and shrieking at the top of her voice?"

"It looks as if some sort of strange battle is about to

take place," said Mr Hobbs, narrowing his eyes slightly as he saw Albert put a whistle to his mouth and produce an ear-deafening blast. Mr Hobbs grabbed Miss Broom's hand: "Come on – let's get out of it – back to civilisation and a couple of ice-creams." Thankfully they turned their backs and wandered across to the chairs and tables outside the park café.

Mr and Mrs Briggs were sitting there too, relaxing after their walk round the park. They were eating choc-ices and Razzle was with them. They nodded politely towards Miss Broom and Mr Hobbs (Dad always nodded when mam nodded, just to be on the safe side).

"Who's that?" grunted dad.

"Miss Broom and Mr Hobbs," hissed mam, keeping a smile on her face. "You've met them loads of times at school … "

Dad shook his head: "There seems to be an unholy row coming from somewhere." He looked at Razzle: "Even the dog can hear it – he's gone all of a quiver."

Razzle was sitting there – his nose raised slightly as he sniffed the air; his ears cocked in alert anticipation. Excitement was afoot … and excitement was just what he needed. It had been an extremely boring afternoon up to now – trying to be a proper town dog taking small dainty steps on this awful prison of a lead round the tulip beds. And not even a reward for good behaviour … not even a sign of getting a lick of that choc-ice.

He tugged gently at his lead, and to his utter delight found it had slipped from mam's hand as she twisted the last remnants of ice-cream from its paper.

With a shrill yelp, Razzle was away!

"Stop him! Stop him!" called mam desperately.

Mr Hobbs could never decide what prompted him to chase after the Briggs's wretched dog on that fateful day, but chase after him he did – with a sudden challenge of energy unknown since his days in the junior rugby league. "The little blighter," he panted to himself, "trust it to belong to those flipping Briggses ... " Mr Hobbs was not going to be beaten by Razzle Briggs even if it *was* rumoured to be the cleverest dog ever to be left in Mr Box's care in the school boiler-room.

The battle was in full swing when Razzle arrived. His tail was wagging twenty to the dozen as he plunged into the yelling mass of howling, hooting bodies all jumping and rolling about round a wooden truck on the grass. Then, with one, loud triumphant yelp – he spotted his rightful lord and master as Jonny emerged in front of Razzle bearing a bulging red balloon full of water, ready to throw at Hobbsey's lot on their trundling truck.

Razzle, barking furiously, leapt towards Jonny with his lead trailing along beside him in the grass. And close on the dangling lead came an outstretched arm as Mr Hobbs flung himself forward to try to grasp Razzle's lead and make him captive again. "Gotcha! You little devil!" muttered Mr Hobbs as his fingers caught the lead at last.

WHOOSH!

WHAM!

SWOOSH!

It was as if the waters of the heavens had broken round poor Mr Hobbs's ears as Jonny and all the rest of Miss Broom's brigade let fire with their water balloons towards the truck with whoops and war cries. Then with a few wet, soggy kites dragging along on strings across the trampled grass they rushed in winning glory to the far end of the battle field, near the park gates.

"We've won!" they gulped breathlessly. "We've won the kite battle against Hobbsey's secret weapon. We've won against their giant Man O' War!"

They all began to flop down on the grass and roll about and laugh uncontrollably, with water pouring down wet cheeks and soaking hair.

Jonny sat up and looked to see what had happened. Was the truck bogged down in that muddy patch made by all their water balloons? Then his face fell . . .

"Get up and GO!" he gasped as he glimpsed the drenched figure of Mr Hobbs staggering angrily towards them all – with Razzle on a lead.

'KEEP ON RUNNING," panted Jonny, as they ran and ran straight out of the park gates.

Eventually they stood panting almost to death outside the Dorman Museum. Then, waving each other goodbye, they all split up and dashed home in fear and triumph.

About two hours later, mam and dad arrived from their afternoon in the park.

"I didn't know quite what to think about our Albert's Extravaganza," said mam doubtfully as she began to get the tea ready. "The place seemed very noisy and there were a lot of children there from your school, Jonny – having a sort of battle. Oh ... and that little pest Razzle escaped whilst dad and I were having an ice-cream. He was rescued by Mr Hobbs from your school. He didn't say much – but he looked very wet."

Jonny looked at her expressionlessly. He was secretly feeling really proud they'd managed to beat Hobbsey's lot with the water balloons. It was a pity it all had to be kept a secret.

"You seem very quiet, love," said mam, as she and dad and Jonny had some tea on their own. "What were you doing all afternoon then? Didn't you see Albert's Extravaganza?"

"I did see some of it," admitted Jonny, then, to take the attention from his own goings on he said: "I met the twins from school and they asked Albert for his autograph and he signed the backs of their hands."

"Poor little souls," said mam. "I hope it'll scrub off all right."

The last week of the school holidays seemed a bit tame after all the battle excitement, and now that Jonny's proper rabbit kite was finished and still resting in the front room behind a chair he began to look forward to going back to school again and taking part in the proper kite contest. There was also Benny Buck to bring back from Marilyn's.

"I'll nip down really early next Tuesday when you go back and give you a lift," said Marilyn helpfully. "Then you'll be able to sit in the back of the Mini with Benny, and we can put your kite in the boot."

The whole school was agog with excitement, as soon the entire playground was a mass of colourful, bobbing, home-made kites of every size, colour and shape.

"Doesn't it look fantastic?" breathed Pam. "There's been a message passed round that we've all got to go straight into the hall first with our kites, and to see that our names are on them and put them all on the chairs. Then Mr Badger and Mr Hobbs and Mr Box are going to choose the best ones and let us know in the classrooms before we go back to collect them again."

Everyone took their kites then filed back to the classroom. Some people were even chewing their nails with excitement, as they pretended to get on with some work.

About fifteen minutes later Mr Badger himself arrived at the classroom door, but as he opened it – Jonny's spirits sank. Mr Hobbs was there as well …

"As you know," explained Mr Badger, "we shall be having our full kite display tomorrow afternoon – to which your parents are all invited – but now I am about to announce the winners in each class, and the Winning Wonder of the whole school ... "

"The winner for this class is the combined effort of twins Jinny and Josie Longshaw who for some reason have tried really hard to make a kite which is like no other kite I have ever seen ... "

Miss Broom smiled at them: "I told them to try and make something which wasn't copied from anyone else's work," she said, "and they seem to have done."

For once, the twins were absolutely stunned by their good fortune and even a bit sad that they couldn't yell that it wasn't fair ...

"Did you have anything in mind when you made it?" asked Mr Badger tactfully.

"Only a Christmas pudding with custard, sir," said Josie. Then when everyone started to laugh she added with a scowl: "Well, it's no dafter than that rabbit one of Jonny Briggs!"

Jonny's enthusiasm fell to rock bottom. The *time*, the *energy*, the *thought* he'd spent on his own kite. The care he'd taken trying to draw the actual face of Benny Buck. The help he managed to get from all the family. And now – this awful disappointment. Those copying, crafty twins – winning for their class with a spotty Christmas pudding covered in yellow custard! It was unbelievable. There were loads better than that. What about Pam's, even? He slumped down sadly in his desk ...

"And that is just what I'm coming to next," said

Mr Badger, beaming. "Because this class has done exceedingly well, and worked amazingly hard on this kite project, and with the casting vote of Mr Box, we have decided to award the top Winning Wonder Kite School prize to Jonny Briggs for his rabbit kite."

The whole class cheered and clapped like mad and Miss Broom's face was like a lobster as she wiped a tear from her cheek. "How really wonderful," she said.

Then everyone turned and looked at Benny Buck resting in his hutch near the Nature table and clapped again.

Jonny Briggs walked home that day in a complete daze. He went over and over it in his mind: how he had actually won the school kite prize after all. It was unbelievable!

But the following day when the parents were there looking at the display and he was standing shyly well away from his own exhibit, he suddenly heard two voices murmuring to each other.

The man's voice was saying: "No one deserves the honour more than you do, Kathleen, and I was pleased in the end. Those twins in your class are fine girls and their Christmas pudding was excellent – but honestly – could you *really* have expected *me* to vote for that awful little wretch Briggs? After all there were hundreds just as good ... And I didn't take kindly to being drenched with water due to his scruffy little dog, that day in the park. All I can say is he can be glad he's on good terms with Mr Box. Mr Box is the one he can really thank." Then their voices faded away as they began to discuss the subjects closest to their hearts.

"Central heating and venetian blinds . . . " smiled Jonny, as he moved quickly away to find Pam.

Winning Wonder! What a title! And he gave a small skip of happiness.

Then, as he reached Pam he said: "How about you and me meeting in the park tomorrow to fly our kites? Just the two of us, and Razzle?"

And that's exactly what they did.